JUSTIFY

kristin harte

Justify: A Vigilante Justice Novel
Copyright © 2017 by Kristin Harte

Paperback ISBN: 978-1-944336-54-7
EBook ISBN: 978-1-944336-53-0
Large Print Hardcover ISBN: 978-1-954702-05-9

This is a work of fiction. Names, places, businesses, characters and incidents are either the product of the author's imagination or are used in a fictitious manner. Any resemblance to actual persons living or dead, actual events or locales is purely coincidental.

Edited by Silently Correcting Your Grammar, LLC

Cover by Kinship Press

For inquiries contact Kristin@KristinHarte.com

JUSTIFY

kristin harte

Chapter One

GAGE

Harvesting lumber was hard work. Having a piece of machinery you needed to complete the job go down made harvesting lumber damn near impossible. And lying in the dirt under that broken piece of machinery—the one that had eight-inch-wide blades on each side of the clamps currently stuck in position on a two-hundred-pound log right above my head— made me an idiot of epic proportions.

It also made me the head heavy machinery mechanic for Kennard Mills.

"We're getting fuel in the radiator up here."

I cursed, wishing my site mechanic would stop pointing out the problems in the engine. I already knew about them, which was why I had crawled underneath the damn thing in the first place. "Yep. I'm waiting on the new injector cups from the supply house."

Hunter—the best site mechanic I had, even though he was

barely more than a high school graduate—sounded almost as shocked as I would have expected him to be. "They still make parts for this thing?"

Not really, no, but there was a strong secondary market for them. I could understand his surprise—I'd have balked the same way had I not worked on these machines every day for the past five years. They looked rough, their bodies showing their age in dents and scratches and the occasional patch of rust we'd have to sand down and seal over. Hell, the delimber had rolled off the assembly line only two years after I'd been born, and I wasn't some young kid. The machine should have been replaced already, but the men knew it well and could work a log through it in a matter of seconds. And while the outside looked beat to hell and back, the motor ran strong and sure... Most of the time.

"Hunter," I snapped as I tried for the tenth time to get a hose connected. Damn thing was up in a squirrel trap of parts and wires. My hands were a bit too big to work the pieces into place, but I couldn't have one of my guys do it. The delimber needed to be moved off the slope it had died on, and there was a log still jammed in the grips. This thing was one good wind away from rolling down the hill and taking whoever was working on it with it. No fucking way was I letting my guys risk their lives that way.

Hunter leaned down to get a look under the rig. "What do you need, boss?"

A beer, a medium rare steak, and a night with a particular brunette. None of which I could have right then. "Pliers. Grab a couple of pairs of needle-nose from my box."

"On it."

As he hurried off on my errand, I let my arms drop to the forest floor. Screw the mud—my shoulder was screaming from holding my arm straight up in the air for the last twenty minutes. I obviously needed to hit the gym a little harder. My physical therapist—the one the military had assigned to me after a bullet had torn through most of my right shoulder joint—would have called me crazy. He'd wanted me to restrict the weight I lifted. Had told me to accept the limitations of my fucked-up arm. I'd refused to be limited by scar tissue and bone fragments.

Ever since I'd gotten out of the SEALs, I'd made sure to rehab my arm and work to get it back to normal. Five years of building muscle and increasing flexibility, of pushing past the pain and fighting to get back to full strength. I wasn't there yet...might never be, but I'd adjusted. My muscles were solid, the weight I could lift more than before the injury. My endurance could obviously use some attention, though. Giving me the next goal to work toward.

Rex—my canine partner in crime and one of the smartest damn dogs on the planet in my humble opinion—lay down and shimmied under the delimber, whining softly as he tried to move closer to my side. His ears perked up when I looked his way, his eyes brightening.

"You know better than to be under here." His head dropped at my tone. I reached out and scratched his ears, hating for him to look so unhappy. He was a good dog, just a bit needy. Damn thing stuck to me like Velcro. Usually, I didn't mind—most people in town had gotten used to the mutt always being by my side. On the job site, though, there were places he couldn't go. Underneath an old logging delimber resting in a precarious position and jammed with a log that weighed over five times what he did was one of them.

"Here you go," Hunter said as he bent down to see under the body of the delimber and handed me the needle-nose pliers. "Hey, Rex. Should he be under there?"

Not in the least. "Rex, go. Guard Hunter."

The dog huffed but did as he was told, crawling out from

under the machine to stand at Hunter's side. Guarding the kid. As he'd continue doing until I called him off.

Seriously, smartest dog in the world.

Shoulder still screaming but not willing to stop because of it, I went back to work. It took about fifteen minutes of prying, tugging, and cursing a blue streak for me to get the hose clamp seated correctly. Another five to finish putting things back together so I could test the engine. Twenty minutes of burning, agonizing pain.

But if the thing started up, it would be worth it.

Moment of truth.

"Let's see if she'll turn over, Hunter."

Within seconds, the old engine roared to life, the big clamps above me sliding down the length of the log and slicing off all the limbs from the main trunk. Exactly as it was built to do.

"Cut it off," I yelled, my ears thankful when the engine quieted once more. "You gave me a run for my money, didn't you, old girl?"

I fell back to the forest floor again, giving myself one quick moment of satisfaction before pushing myself out from underneath the rig. I needed a beer after that job. Not that I'd have one anytime soon. Kennard crews were working double shifts at the Hansen harvest site. A rough monsoon season and a motorcycle gang fucking with us had delayed our efforts, and the weather reporters were all calling for an early snow season. We needed to get the trees felled, the limbs stripped, the logs loaded, and the trucks back down the mountain to the mill before winter hit. That meant time was short.

Once on my feet again, I pointed at Hunter. "Go tell Camden she's back up and running. Rex, heel."

My dog responded immediately, running to my side. Hunter did not. In face, he looked uncomfortable as he paused before sighing and bounding toward the site manager—the one I wouldn't have wanted to talk to either. Dead eyes, haggard appearance, and enough bad attitude to feel it from fifty yards away, the guy wasn't looking his best. I couldn't blame him for that, though.

Camden Reese. Site manager for Kennard Mills, former Marine, friend of the Kennard family practically since birth, and recent widower. A motorcycle club called The Soul Suckers had burned his house down after he'd found them in the woods by our job site. Turned out, they'd been cooking meth out there, and we'd gotten in their way. They'd struck hard and killed Camden's wife in the process. They'd also destroyed one of the best men I'd ever met in doing so.

But we'd gotten them back for that, me and Alder Kennard, the man in charge of the mill. We'd retaliated one night in Alder's barn when more Soul Suckers had shown up. If anyone ever tried to tell me those two guys who'd come for Alder hadn't deserved to die, I'd simply remind them one of them had helped light that fire and taken a good woman from our community. The community the Kennard family had been tasked with protecting. The people I'd lay down my life for. I might not have been a Kennard by blood, but the second son of the family was more my brother than any blood relative could be, so I did my best to live up to the expectations placed on their shoulders.

As I sat on a fallen log with Rex beside me, my phone rang. It took me a second to recognize the song playing, but when I did, I knew exactly who was on the other end of the line. No one else would put a seventies ballad as their ringtone.

I didn't need to greet the motherfucker with anything more polite than, "What is this shit song, and why is it on my phone?"

Bishop—best friend, former SEAL teammate, and all-around

pain in my ass—laughed. "Stephen Bishop's *It Might Be You* is a classic. You should listen to it."

"Last time I checked, I still had my balls. So, no."

"Don't worry—I'll call you every five minutes and let it ring so you can go deep with the earworm."

He would, too. "I can't believe you fucked with my phone again."

"I can't believe it took you this long to figure that out."

"It's the twenty-first century—who calls people?"

"I like to be unique."

"What you like to be is a jackass, jackass. Why are you calling? Shouldn't you be busy doing things to your girl that are illegal in some states?"

"Is that jealousy I hear in your tone, Gage?"

It might have been, but fuck if I'd admit that. I was actually glad Bishop had hooked back up with his ex-girlfriend. Thrilled, really. These past few weeks with Anabeth, he'd been happier than I'd ever seen him in all the years we'd known each other. Not that I got to see him much—Anabeth worked as an entertainer in Vegas reading tea leaves and tarot cards and shit. Bishop had been spending more than half his time out there since they'd jumped back into a relationship. Good thing, too. The Soul Suckers had a score to settle with her, one we'd blocked once already. They'd taken her hostage on my watch, sneaking past me and busting into her house before I'd known they were there. We'd gotten her out alive, but it'd been close. Close enough for a heavy ball of lead to sit in my gut whenever I thought about the mistakes I'd made that night. Never again.

"I'm not jealous, man. But I know what I'd be doing if I had a woman by my side who looked like your Legs."

Though I didn't want a woman like Legs—tall, with big blue eyes and long, red hair. No, I wanted a woman who was short and curvy with dark hair and hazel eyes. I wanted her bad. But having a hard-on at a job site was probably a bad idea, so I kept the thoughts of that woman tucked away as deep as I could. Just like every other day since she'd shown up in Justice.

Bishop just laughed. Again. "Keep calling her that, and she'll strike back at you one of these days."

"I await the battle of words. Now, really…what's up?"

His joking tone changed, grew more serious. "I'm not coming back this week."

"Staying in Vegas again?"

"Yeah. Anabeth got a last-minute gig at some awards show, and there's a bike rally outside the city."

He didn't mean Schwinns. "Seen any of our friends there?"

"There's been a few vests on the strip."

The Soul Suckers were a national club, so that didn't surprise me. Didn't mean any of them was from the branch one county to the west of us or the one causing trouble down in Boulder, but the possibility was there. "Better not to risk leaving her alone if they're that close."

"That's my thought, too. So you've got my place to yourself for another week."

Because I'd been living with him while I remodeled an old cabin I'd bought over the summer. "No problem. I'll take care of things."

"Keep your dog off my couch."

I tilted my head at Rex, grinning when he mimicked me. "I don't think you need to worry about your couch. He's been sleeping on your bed."

"You'd better be fucking with me."

Maybe. Maybe not. But I sure did like pushing Bishop's buttons. "I'd wash your pillows when you get back if I were you. He likes to plant his ass right in the middle of them."

"I will kick both of you out if I find a single dog hair on my pillows."

I held the phone away from my mouth, making a static sound by blowing air over my teeth. "What's that? SSSHHHHHHH. You're break—SSSHHHHHH—up. Can't—SSSSSHHHHH—you."

"You're a jerk, Gage Shepherd. Tell my brother I'll call him later."

"Will do." I brought the phone back to my ear. "Watch your back, man. And if you need someone else to watch it for you—"

"I'll call. Have fun not talking to Katie."

Before I could fire back, he hung up. Of course. Typical Bishop—lob one last softball and make a quick exit. And the one he'd lobbed at me?

Katie. As in Baker. As in niece to our corrupt county sheriff, recently moved back home to Justice from Denver, and chef-owner of a new restaurant in town. As in the short, curvy, brown-haired princess I'd been lusting after since the first day I met her. Bishop knew about my obsession even though I'd never said anything. Knew and pushed me to do something about it all the damn time. But every time those big hazel eyes met mine, I could almost see the nerves flaring inside of her. I scared her, and that didn't bode well for me getting a date.

As I tucked my phone back into my pocket, Camden whistled loudly.

"That's it," he yelled, looking more pissed than I'd ever seen him. "Let's call it a day."

The loggers all packed up their tools and began heading toward the mill's ATVs that would take them back to their cars parked about two miles south of the ridge. Many of them would end up going to The Baker's Cottage for dinner. Katie's place. Like most of our employees, I ate there quite often. I was no

Alder Kennard—sitting in a diner booth every night just to get a peek of the girl I was interested in for three long years—but that was only because I hadn't known the owner for three years. If I had...

Yeah, I owed Alder an apology for mocking him as badly as I did all those years.

Still, The Baker's Cottage had great food, and it was the only restaurant actually in Justice. Even without the presence of Katie, I'd have probably eaten there almost daily. She was just a bonus—or maybe a punishment. Too fucking perfect for me to ignore and way too sweet to be with a guy like me. Something that irritated me to no end.

I might have been too much for her—between my long, thick hair, my full beard, and the ink running from my wrists to my neck, she wouldn't have been the only woman put off by my appearance. She was just the first one whose disapproval bothered me.

And as such, I was thinking I could make a few concessions for her. Cut my hair, trim my beard—neaten up my overall look. Tame the mountain man thing I had going on. I couldn't get rid of the tattoos, not that I wanted to, but I could clean up. The guys would roast me for it, but if those simple things might help me get my hands—and potentially other parts—on those killer curves I practically drooled over? It'd be worth the ribbing.

I'd have to figure out how to talk to her, too. I mean, I knew how to talk—she wasn't the first woman I'd ever wanted to pick up. But around her, my thoughts turned too dirty, too base. She talked about the food she made and what was happening in town, while all I could think of was how sweet her pussy would be on my tongue and if she was a screamer when she came. I wanted to find out. Needed to. Hard to do when I couldn't open my mouth for fear of scaring her off with how much I wanted to get her naked.

When Camden finally came up the hill—the last man to leave the site—I gave him a fist bump and followed him toward the ATVs.

"You coming to The Baker's Cottage with us?"

Camden shook his head, looking tired and downright mean. "I'm heading home."

Which meant driving to where his house used to be and getting drunk in his car. I knew. I didn't say much, but I knew.

"Gonna snow soon," I said, keeping my eyes forward and my steps even. "You won't be able to live in your car much longer."

Camden's angry expression darkened farther, and his words hit like fists as he said, "I don't need you telling me what I can or can't do, Shepherd."

Okay then. I whistled for Rex to follow me and climbed onto the four-wheeler I'd driven to the site, leaving Camden to deal with his own exit but keeping close enough to watch him. I'd never leave a man behind, but I also couldn't help someone who didn't want to be helped. Some men needed to hit rock bottom before being willing to move forward in life. I'd figured living in a car outside the burned-out shell of a house where the woman he'd loved had been murdered would have been Camden's rock bottom—I'd been wrong.

So I let his words rest, knowing the guy was torn up by his loss. Rock bottom would come eventually. I could only hope one of us would be around to pick him back up when it did.

I drove behind Camden through the woods, Rex running along beside me. When we made it to the landing where we'd load the logs for their trip to the mill, I parked the vehicle and grabbed a towel from my truck. I was dirtier than my dog, but I knew better than to put my filthy paws on the upholstered seats. Rex did not, so he got rubbed down to remove the worst of the mess. If I were smart, I'd have headed back to Bishop's to grab a shower and some clean clothes before seeing Katie. Make myself presentable and all that.

I wasn't smart.

I was impatient.

And I was starving, just not for food.

I'd been in the kitchen with Katie when she'd been covered in flour, elbow deep in raw meat, and sweating as if she'd run a marathon. I still wanted to get my hands on her every second of every day. Even more, really—that passion she had for her work was too fucking attractive to resist. Katie could see me just as I was—end-of-shift dirty with my hair tied back and the ink on my neck on full display.

I'd be in the shower enough tonight once I left her place. Me and Righty had a standing date because if I wasn't getting any from Katie, I wasn't getting any from anyone else. I was a one-woman man, and that woman had no clue I was already wrapped around her little finger.

Chapter Two

KATIE

In a normal restaurant, the dinner rush would be served over the course of a couple of hours as diners came in small groups. You could plan for that, could find the time to do things well if you prepped and stuck to your process.

In a logging town, the dinner rush was one single sixty-minute period when every customer you'd have for a night would hit the door at once. That fact meant each night I threw everything I'd ever learned about running a kitchen out the window and prayed I'd make it through dessert.

"Alder texted. The crew's been released. They'll be coming down the mountain within twenty minutes." Shye—one of my waitresses and a woman becoming a pretty good friend to me—raced through the kitchen, grabbing supplies to finish prepping the tables. Her blond hair sat piled high on her head—the only thing *high* about the shorter-than-average woman. Not that I was any better. With both of us topping out at barely five feet tall, we'd been forced to keep a couple of shelves empty or else we wouldn't have been able to reach them when we were the only two working. Which happened a lot. Not tonight, though—we had an extra waitress to run the floor in case I needed Shye's help cooking.

Because once the loggers showed up, there would be no stopping for me.

"Thank you, Shye. Make sure the updated menus are on the tables. No sense making the guys wait for them."

"On it." She disappeared through the door with a smile on her face. Alder—her big, burly boyfriend—would hit the door first for sure. He owned the mill, so he could leave whenever he wanted. He also hated to be away from Shye, and he made sure to grab a few extra minutes to say hello when they were rejoined. His version of hello involved lots of kissing and wandering hands, whispered words of sweetness, and a definite promise of the naughty that would come later. In other words, their hellos were something to avoid watching.

Not that I saw anything wrong with a little PDA. To be honest, I wanted the same sort of connection with a man—who wouldn't?—just not with *that* man. Alder was too tame, too controlled, too safe. I wanted rough and strong, the kind of man that set your panties on fire and made you a little nervous.

A tough man with a heart of gold. An impossible dream it had always seemed, until... *Focus, woman.*

Food. That had to be my priority for the night. I took a breath to clear my head and thought through my menu for the evening. I could do this; I could stay on task and on target. I just had to ignore the distractions bombarding me. With nothing on my mind but making my diners happy, I grabbed a knife and started cutting more potatoes to boil and mash. Paring back on what I offered had become a necessity because of how the dinner rush worked in Justice. Four offerings tonight, things I knew the men loved, plus a special homemade gnocchi in marinara sauce that made the couple of kids in town happy. That was it—no special orders, no substitutions, and hopefully, no complaining.

When I had the potatoes in the water, I gave my kitchen another quick, sweeping glance. My prep work seemed complete —meat either roasting or ready to go, vegetables par-cooked, water boiling in two pots for the gnocchi, sauces made, plates lined up and ready to be filled. I had this.

I'd been in the weeds every night since my grand opening celebration. The dinner rush continued to grow and become more demanding, which wasn't a bad thing. Business was good, which should have thrilled me, but the rush every night left me frustrated and exhausted more than satisfied. I'd broken down and hired another person for the kitchen—a lady from Rock Falls with restaurant experience as a line cook. She'd help me up my game and get food out faster, but she wouldn't be in the kitchen tonight. It was just me. Me and the annoying little order printer that never quieted. Me and a hundred people filling my dining room all within a five-minute stretch. Me and my food that couldn't get plated fast enough.

One night. Give me one night where I don't lose control of this kitchen. I need to prove I can do this.

But prayers wouldn't help me. Not with this. I loved cooking, loved feeding people good, wholesome meals I knew would fuel them well. I loved it even more now that I was feeding my hometown in a restaurant I ran with staff I had chosen under the watchful eye of the Kennard family. I'd liked being a chef when I'd lived in Denver, but nothing would ever replace the feeling of working in my own kitchen, in my own restaurant, in the town where I grew up. Where I felt safe and at home.

Let the loggers come. I could handle the rush.

I cracked my neck. "You've got this."

Shye burst through the doors. "The trucks are coming down Main Street."

She grabbed a full tray of water glasses from the walk-in and headed out to the dining room to finalize the tables. Leaving me with my food. Exactly where I was meant to be.

The sound of the bell over the restaurant entrance door and the deep bass of the men chatting as they entered broke the relative silence of the kitchen. My heart jumped, stuttered, made itself known inside my chest. The hussy.

As much as I hated thinking about him when I had so many other things to focus on, I couldn't help but wonder if Gage Shepherd—heavy machinery mechanic for Kennard Mills and a bear of a man with the darkest eyes I'd ever seen—was out there already. If he'd be coming in tonight. The man drove my nerves to the brink like no one else—something in the way his very presence commanded a room making my heart want to leap out of my chest every time I was around him. I tended to talk when I got nervous. A lot. As in babble or word vomit. I'd done that to him too many times to count, which was why I tried to ignore him. To stay away from that big, dark, bearded brute of a man. But tonight felt different. *I* felt different. I wouldn't let my fear of him overwhelm me this time. I would stand my ground instead of running when he showed up. This was my place, my business. My kitchen.

I could control myself in front of Gage Shepherd.

But deep down, I knew that was a pipe dream. Just like my kitchen during the dinner rush, I lost control around him. I did my best—tried to chat, tried to sound normal—but eventually, the flutters in my tummy and the way my heart pounded so hard would get the better of me, and I'd embarrass myself before running away to hide. I couldn't help it. He was just so...big and domineering. One glance, and he threw every instinct I had for self-preservation into overdrive while making me want to curl up against his broad chest and wrap myself around him at the same time.

Fear and desire didn't go together, did they?

The order printer came to life, spewing ticket after ticket of orders as my two waitresses did their jobs in the dining room. It was time to do mine. My brain had no room for thoughts of Gage Shepherd until that machine stopped spitting out orders.

"I will not fall behind tonight."

———

Thirty minutes. From nothing to a full dining room completely served in thirty minutes. My hands hurt, my shoulders burned, and my throat felt raw from yelling directions at my two-person staff, but I'd done it. I'd made it through without falling behind.

I stood in my kitchen, listening to the rumble of the diners in the other room, giving myself a moment to catch my breath before I checked on my guests. Those men out there knew me, had known my family. Most had watched me grow up in Justice. I had to make an appearance no matter how much I wanted to fall into the chair in my office and take a nap. So I took a deep breath, rolled my neck one last time, and I looked up.

And promptly screamed.

"Jesus, Gage." My hand rested over my heart as if trying to hold the organ in place as it attempted to beat its way out of my chest. "You scared me."

He always did, but I refused to admit that to him. The man in question stood across the room in a corner with his dog Rex at his side. A common sight around town, those two. Gage's long, thick hair looked to be pulled back from his face, and his beard hung just as bushy as ever. A dark cloud decorating his face, almost hiding him. The man was made of shadows, slipping into spaces without anyone noticing. But when they did, when I did, I couldn't focus on anything other than his darkness—almost black eyes, hair the shade of burnt timber, even his skin held on to a golden sort of color year-round. At least, the parts not covered in colorful ink.

Made of shadows indeed—deep ones. Ones a girl like me should avoid.

"I didn't mean to scare you." Gage cocked his head and drew his eyebrows together. Frowning. Unhappy with the statement I'd made, it seemed. Something that fired up my nerves and pushed me past the point of being able to control myself. As usual.

I clutched a kitchen towel, slowly wringing it with shaking hands. "I didn't mean *scared* scared. At least not scared like *OMG, there's an axe murderer in my kitchen*—have you ever seen that *So I Married an Axe Murderer* movie? Super funny. My mom really liked it, so I've probably watched it a thousand times over the years. It was a Thanksgiving tradition, actually. That and the weird canned cranberry sauce she refused to give up no matter how many times I brought homemade to dinner. Nothing natural wiggles like that canned stuff. Anyway, yeah—not axe murderer scared. More scared like startled. Or spooked. Spooked is a good word for how I just felt. Surprised works, too. I looked up, and there you were. Poof. Like magic. I wasn't expecting you to be there, though I guess I should have expected it. You being there, I mean. You're *there* enough that I should be used to it, but...I wasn't. Tonight."

Shut up, Katie.

His eyebrows said so much more than he ever did. Especially when he raised them the way he just had. When they lifted his face a bit and opened those dark eyes wider. The ones still pinning me in place. As if trying to see through me. Trying to compel me to do something with just a look.

"So, I'm always there...but I scared you because I was there."

Oh god, I was going to have a full-on panic attack if he didn't stop looking at me.

I wrung my towel harder, tighter, unable to hold still. Needing to keep my hands busy. "Okay, *always* may have been an exaggeration. You're not always here. Just a lot. You and Camden seem to get stuck with guarding Main Street more than the others. I'm sorry—that's such a waste of your time. But I get it, you know? Someone has to look out because of the Soul Suckers trouble. Totally understandable. You sort of have to be here. It's not like—"

"Hey, Katie." His voice rumbled through the kitchen, stealing my breath and making my knees quiver.

"Yeah?"

"Hi." He smiled. Oh my god, he *smiled*. At me. And...I lost my damn mind.

"Hi."

Did...did I just sigh that? I clamped my jaws together, refusing to speak more. Already dying on the inside. Why couldn't I be normal around the guy? I got nervous and I babbled, yes. Absolutely. Always had, but nothing like what happened around Gage Shepherd. He took my natural nervous tendency and kicked it up to eleven. Meanwhile, he said nothing. Just watched me with those almost-black eyes. Well, I watched him too. And I liked what I saw way too much.

Thick hair, full beard, ink, and muscles—a little scary and a lot sexy. That's what you got with Gage. The man stood out in a crowd for both his size and his wild appearance. An appearance that made me wonder what sort of lips sat under all that hair, what sorts of dips and planes were hidden under those clothes. I'd have bet my restaurant that the man looked amazing with his shirt off.

Too bad I'd likely never find out.

Gage didn't say anything. Not a word. He just stood across the room, Rex sitting calmly beside him like usual, both watching me. Something I'd noticed more and more. I got nervous, babbled, he interrupted me and then said nothing. Giving me time to get control of my nerves. Or maybe he was waiting me out to see if I would fill the silence more. It had to be a big joke—how Katie Baker couldn't stop babbling around him. Professional kitchens were often filled with men, so I knew how they talked. How they joked and teased and mocked. I bet the guys got a good laugh about my silly crush on Gage.

A thought that soured my mood enough to push away the nerves.

"Can I get you something? Are you hungry?"

His eyes turned molten, black liquid watching my every move. A physical caress in a look.

"I could eat." His voice caused tingles to shoot up my spine—always did—but the nerves had faded. This, I could control. Food was easy. There was no rambling when I cooked, no stilted conversations or awkward silences that I felt the need to fill. There was nothing but me and the ingredients and the skills that had been beaten into me over the years.

Cooking, I could do.

"What would you like?"

He smirked. "What will you feed me?"

That shiver returned, the tingles moving through my body to other places, too. Places like the tips of my breasts and the flesh between my legs. His voice might as well have been an aphrodisiac for all it did to me. And the question? What would I feed him?

That sounded dirty. So, so naughty in the best way ever. He had to know that. Or maybe he didn't—maybe he simply never saw me as someone to be naughty with.

I would have to work hard to ignore that thought.

But then…what *would* I feed him? Gage ate anything I put in front of him, but for some reason, I always wanted to do more. Steaks were too easy, and he'd had the meatloaf a few times already. The pulled pork special wouldn't do for him—at least, not on its own. It wasn't original enough. Wasn't in any way wild or different. But I had other options.

"Do you like finger foods?" I asked, ideas sprouting and twisting in my mind as a picture formed. "Nachos?"

Gage nodded, still staring at me. Still making my heart race and parts of me tingle in ways they shouldn't. Or maybe they should. Just not in a kitchen with a man I barely knew.

"Okay," I said, hanging my towel on the prep counter bar and refocusing on the task at hand. "Let's have some fun."

A quick roux, cheese, sliced jalapeños, and a little fresh pico de gallo went into a pot, the sauce coming together in minutes. Longer than I would have liked, but Gage would wait. The man had the patience of a saint, it seemed. He never complained that my changing the menu options and making him something personal took too long. He rarely said a word other than yes and thanks and hi, Katie, in fact.

Once the sauce had set up, I stacked warmed tortilla chips on a large plate, added the shredded pork, some barbecue sauce I'd made that morning, topped it with the cheese sauce, then garnished it all with more jalapeños and pico. A fun dish, a little different way to use the meat, and—I'd bet—delicious.

Yet, for some reason, my hands shook as I set the plate on the counter in front of Gage. "*Bon appetit.*"

He stepped closer, all slow movements and animal grace. No

rush, no extra energy expended. Just one step at a time until he stood on the other side of the counter from me. As if testing the waters, he took just one chip and brought it to his mouth. So slow...building tension with every second that passed. A flash of pink lips and tongue was all I got before the chip disappeared and I waited for the verdict.

And waited.

And...

He groaned, grabbing two more chips before the noise had even died down.

Joy and something else filled me. Something warm and vibrant, smooth like homemade caramel and just as sweet. Something that screamed of desire. I blamed the moan—I about flooded my panties at the sound. A thought that made the butterflies in my tummy come back with a vengeance. The words followed.

"Yeah, so the flavors of the slow roasted pork and the sharpness of the cheese balance well with the saltiness of the chips. The pico is more for texture than anything else because, really, it can't stand up to all those other stronger flavor profiles. Some places use a sweeter barbecue sauce, but I prefer a more mellow type of smokiness on the tongue. So yeah, pulled pork nachos. I'd put this on the menu but the roux takes a long time and making the cheese sauce in batches would cause me to have too much waste, plus the pulled pork plates and sandwiches have a really nice margin and the nachos wouldn't, so I just keep those on the menu instead. Though I guess I could do something like this for weekends. Maybe game days or...but no, I don't have TVs for a sporting event. That won't work. Maybe something else, though. Or should I add some TVs to the bar area? I could probably do that—only turn them on for specific events or something. But then the guys would want to hang out here, and I'm not up for loggerpalooza in my bar area every weekend."

Shut up, shut up, shut up.

I clenched my jaw, my right hand gripping my left as if trying to hold each other in place. The talking, oh my god, the talking. I really needed to work on that. To learn to be quieter around him. The man barely said anything at all, and I babbled endlessly every time we were in the same room. How could he stand the babbling?

Gage just stood there, though. Chewing slowly. Watching me until he found something to say. "These are the best goddamned nachos I've ever had in my life."

Warmth exploded through my chest, and I grinned. "Yeah?"

He held out a chip to me, raising his eyebrows as if asking permission. I didn't even have to think or question him. I simply opened my mouth and let him place the food on my tongue. The intimacy of the act, of him feeding me, didn't hit me until it was too late. We were so close—even with the counter between us—that I could see the bits of dirt on his shirt, the shadows on his face from a hard day's work. I took in every detail, every nuance. Greedily hoarded them for later when I was alone in my little apartment and wondering what he was doing.

But then I bit down, and it was my turn to groan. The texture of the meat and the chip was a delight, and the slight sweetness of the sauce countered the saltiness of the chip. Heat from the jalapeños gave the bite just enough kick to make it interesting, and the cheese sauce had the perfect creaminess to keep everything from being too harsh. Overall, a total win.

"Better than I thought," I said once I'd swallowed. I looked up to find Gage watching me again, his eyes that same liquid darkness I'd noticed earlier. Burning into me. I could have stared into those inky depths for hours, could have gotten lost in them.

Could have begged for him to tell me what that heated look meant because it brought something to life inside of me.

Sadly, I didn't do any of that.

Shye barreled into the kitchen, a grin on her face and a tray in her hands. "Dessert orders should be starting in the next few minutes, and five guys have asked if you're coming out to say hi tonight. Young guys. You seem to have a fan club, Miss Katie." She disappeared into the walk-in freezer, probably to pull the vanilla ice cream for the peach cobbler special. Which reminded me of all the work still to be done.

Spell...broken.

"Duty calls." I shrugged and nodded toward the plate. "Eat up. I'd hate to have that all go to waste."

"I wouldn't waste a bite of your food." He frowned, his heavy brow falling slightly as he did. "Though, I like canned cranberry sauce. I thought only TV chefs attempted homemade."

"I'll make you the real stuff." If he kept looking at me like that, I'd make him an entire Thanksgiving feast just to watch him enjoy it. "Maybe a turkey sandwich special with dressing and cranberry sauce. I'll buy a can, too. Then you can try them at the same time and taste the difference."

"That seems like a lot of work."

I shrugged, knowing it was. Not caring because it meant I could do something for him. "It'd be fun, though."

Gage quirked another smile my way, setting the butterflies fluttering again. But before he could answer me, the printer began spitting out dessert orders.

He nodded at the whining machine. "What's for dessert?"

"Peach cobbler with homemade vanilla ice cream on top. And I made that cinnamon whipped cream you like so much."

"Jesus, I could lick up every drop of your cream." His face suddenly stilled, his eyes darting to mine as if he'd just said something wrong. As if he hadn't meant for those words to slip out.

Meanwhile, I couldn't stop thinking about all the naughty things his tongue could do to my body. About all the things I could do to his. About running my hands over every inch of him and feeling those thick muscles tense as he came. As he lost all that control he seemed to have.

Focus...gone. Luckily, I wasn't a stranger to making normal sentences sound naughty. "At least wait until you've got my peaches in your mouth first. They're amazingly sweet."

His eyes burned into me, making me flush. "I have no doubt about that, princess." He nodded toward my work area, grabbing his plate and stepping back from the counter. Heading toward the door to the dining room. "You'd better get to work."

"Right. Yeah. Dessert."

He grinned again, leaving me even more flustered. "Rex, guard."

And then he was gone, and I was left with his dog, an uncomfortable empty sensation, and wet panties.

And a lot of orders for peach cobbler a la mode.

The muscle memory of setting up plate after plate of cobbler took hold, the concentration necessary to present dessert properly sweeping over me in a calming wave that knocked out everything else. All that was left in my world—all there was room for in my head—was the food, the flavors, and the pretty, pretty hills of sweetness I needed to build.

And if every dark spot I saw reminded me of Gage's eyes, well, that was just a coincidence.

Chapter Three

GAGE

The next morning, I cursed every bump on the way to the job site. How could I not when I was pretty sure I'd jacked off more in the hours after I'd left The Baker's Cottage than I ever had before. Even horny teenager me hadn't gone at it enough to be chafed. Adult me had...all because of nachos and peaches.

Well, really because of soft, pink lips opening so sweetly for me as I placed food between them. I still don't know what I'd been thinking when I'd fed Katie, but thank fuck I had. That picture—those lips parting and taking what I had to give—would be spank bank material for the rest of my life. And when she'd thrown out the comment about eating her peaches? I'd had to leave the room before I pinned her against the counter and got a real good taste of her. One I'd make sure she didn't soon forget.

I cringed as the ATV hit a patch of rock that caused twinges to shoot up my poor, aching dick. I'd truly screwed myself the night before. I'd let myself lose control enough to believe the woman could be mine. No way would I stop now until I had Katie in my bed, which meant I had to up my game and put in some work.

Once I'd arrived on site and parked the ATV, I adjusted myself subtly as I swung my leg off the ATV. I didn't need to be there—wasn't scheduled and didn't have an emergency—but Hunter had needed to take the day off. When I'd taken the call, I'd figured I could pop over and make sure the machinery ran well for the morning shift. Besides, Katie would know something was up if I came by the restaurant so early. I could get some work done before I went bulldogging after her.

The second I took in the logging team, every thought of Katie and those soft, pink lips disappeared. Even my aching dick no longer starred in the front of my mind. With just one glance at Camden, I moved straight into damage control mode and thanked every deity there was that I'd showed up.

Rough no longer described the way he looked. Haggard, sickly, waxy—all better descriptors. His team seemed to be noticing too. They kept shooting worried glances at each other, and one guy seemed to be sticking awfully close to their site manager. I had a feeling if Camden gave them a direction, there'd be a lot of silent conversation before the team decided if it was a good idea or not. And that was a dangerous thing when cutting down trees.

I didn't think twice before grabbing my phone and calling in. Not to Bishop—he handled sales, though he could deal with other issues. No, this one needed to go right to the top. To the big boss running the company. I called Alder Kennard.

He answered on the second ring. "What's up?"

"We've got a problem. It's Camden."

Alder paused, the silence obvious, before carefully asking, "What's the situation?"

I watched Camden interact with Vol, an old-timer who'd been logging these woods since before I'd been born. The old man seemed to be running interference, keeping Camden occupied while the team, led by Vol's son, shifted positions. It looked to me as if Camden had been headed for the skidder.

All the felled timber had to be pulled out of the forest to the landing site for loading onto the trucks that would take it to the mill. That was the job of the skidder—a giant piece of machinery with a boom and grapple bucket to grab, lift, and pull the logs off the site. The beast scarred the earth beneath it and could take out the whole team if the operator didn't pay attention to what they were doing. Vol always paid attention, but I doubted Camden could focus on his own hand if he had to right then.

And Camden? He looked like my dad. Not literally—the two were physically as opposite as possible—but similar in how they acted. My dad had been an alcoholic, a functioning one, but an addict nonetheless. I knew the look of someone who was still burning off the night before. My dad had worn it often, and there was Camden doing the same. It was a "been drinking all night but trying to appear sober" sort of look. One that should be nowhere near a logging operation.

There was no sugarcoating that shit. "Camden's been drinking."

"How bad?" Alder's voice no longer seemed cautious. He sounded pissed as hell.

"I'm having to guess here, but bad enough that I'm about to siphon the diesel out of the skidder to keep him from running it."

"Don't let him touch a goddamned thing. I'm on my way."

Right. Don't let the site manager touch the equipment. No problem there.

"Yo, Rusty," I hollered once I'd pocketed my phone. The man in question looked up then hurried over at my wave. He fit his nickname—Rusty had a shock of dark red hair on the top of his head and covering half his face and a smattering of freckles across his pale skin. The kid was our newest employee—a silviculturist working with the crew to make sure we left the forest healthier than when we started. He knew the business well, was quick and smart in an unsafe environment, and he had the reputation of being observant. Real fucking observant.

Tall and thick with muscle, he powered up the rocky rise in no time. "What's up, Gage?"

"You notice any issues on site this morning?"

A single jaw clench gave him away. "Nothing that hasn't already been brought up and squashed."

So the team was sticking behind their leader. I liked loyalty, but I didn't like stupidity. "Cam been using the machinery?"

"No. Old Vol's been making sure of it."

Just like I'd thought. Vol knew this job better than anyone in the company, including Alder himself. He'd been friends with the late Kennard patriarch back in the day. His been-there-done-that attitude tended to settle the young hotheads we hired, and he took good care of his team, especially when his son worked with him. He should have been retired by now, but at that moment, I was real fucking thankful he hadn't.

Rusty wasn't who I needed to talk to. "Okay. Get back to work and send Vol over."

The two switched spots, Rusty keeping close to Camden as the old man left his side. Real observant, that one. He'd be a good man to put on rotation for guarding Main Street.

"What can I do for you, Gage?" Vol asked when he stood on the hunk of rock at my side.

I'd needed to go easy on Rusty. Vol required no such thing. "You letting Cam lead this site like he is?"

"I've got him covered."

"You shouldn't need to cover your site manager."

"Yeah, well, he shouldn't have lost his wife either."

True fact, and yet... "You going to cover for him when he kills another teammate because he's too drunk to react?"

A flash of something close to worry flashed across his face, but it disappeared just as quickly. "We take care of our own in Justice, and Cam needs a little extra help right now."

I could respect that opinion. I didn't like it because I could already see how badly this day could go if they lost control for just a moment, but I could respect it. Loyalty above all else—if I hadn't have known better, I'd have guessed Vol had been a SEAL.

"Okay. Keep doing what you're doing. I'm here if you need backup, and Alder's on his way."

Vol nodded, looking relieved as he headed back to work. Logging was dangerous work on a good day—between the machinery, the locations, and the simple physics of felling 200-foot-tall trees, accidents were inevitable. No one wanted a team member to go down on their shift, though. Not even someone trying to show an old friend some compassion.

I hung back from the team, watching over them as they worked on the felled timber. Had they been dropping trees, I'd have put a stop to the whole operation. Cutting off the limbs and readying the timber to be yarded to the landing site was a lot less dangerous. Still, I stuck around, keeping an eye on Camden as he *sort of* did his job. He knew I was there, had caught my gaze once or twice, but he made no move to acknowledge me. Fucker had to know he was busted.

Alder arrived a good half hour after I'd called, pulling up on an ATV like the rest of the guys did. "No accidents?"

"None yet."

"Fucking drunk at work. What is he thinking?"

"He's not." I shrugged when Alder looked my way. "He's

grieving. Thinking isn't his highest priority. Trying to figure out if he wants to live through the pain or not is."

"Yeah, well...a drunk on a job site could lead to a lot more people grieving. I can't have it."

No, he couldn't.

Alder stormed off toward Camden, pulling him aside and indicating Vol should take over for a few. I moved close enough to listen, to back Alder up if he needed it, but not so close as to interfere. Dealing with disciplinary actions against employees of Kennard Mills wasn't part of my job. Making sure Alder made it back down off the mountain was.

"Are you fucking kidding me?" Camden yelled, obviously having lost his temper. Alder must have told him he knew he'd been drinking. I couldn't hear both sides of the conversation—Alder kept his voice low and controlled—but Camden was loud enough for the both of them.

"Yeah, I had a few drinks last night. So what?"

"I'm fine. I can do my goddamned job just fine, too."

"Right. You're so worried about everyone. You weren't too worried about Leah, were you?"

That one...I knew it hit Alder hard. As the oldest Kennard brother, he was tasked with taking care of the town. We didn't have police or fire departments this far out into the hills. With fewer than 350 residents, the city of Justice couldn't afford them anyway, so the Kennard family handled those jobs themselves.

When Camden's wife, Leah, had died in that fire set by the Soul Suckers, it'd broken something inside of Camden. It'd broken something inside of Alder as well. And Camden had just ground all those broken pieces with his boot, purposely causing pain.

Alder stayed solid, though. Quiet. Looking like a leader. Camden wasn't wanting to be led.

"Fuck you and your whole family. You didn't do shit for me. You didn't keep Leah safe. You fucking failed, and I lost the one woman I'll ever give a fuck about because of it."

Alder reached for Cam, but the younger man shoved him back. That was quite literally my cue to step in.

"Keep your hands off him," I said, making sure I had Cam's attention. "Say what you need to, but don't get physical."

Camden's bloodshot eyes met mine, his anger palpable. "Fuck you, Shepherd."

"That's enough," Alder said, but Cam wasn't listening. In fact, he pulled off his fluorescent safety vest instead.

"You know what?" Camden asked just before he tossed the vest at Alder. "I'm done here. Fuck this job and your mill. Fuck this whole town. I quit, and I'm leaving Justice. Good luck against the Soul Suckers. Hope they don't murder your woman like they did mine. Oh, right—you'll actually do something to stop them from getting to Shye. Leah wasn't important enough to you."

Alder's face fell, the pain those words caused obvious. Camden may have been grieving, but he was also an asshole for that one. Before I could do much more than get pissed, though, Camden stormed off up the hill. Heading for the vehicles that would take him back to his truck.

"Camden," Alder yelled. "Go sleep it off at Deacon's motel before you lock that decision down. You'll always be family to us."

Camden didn't respond. I couldn't let him leave drunk, though.

"Rusty," I hollered, moving away from Alder and waiting until the redhead stood close enough to give him directions. "Go with him. Make sure he doesn't kill anyone else, even if that means following his truck all the way to the county line."

"And if he's out of control?"

Fuck. Alder would never approve what I was about to say, but no way could I let Camden kill someone else because he'd drunk too much. If it were up to me, I wouldn't have let him leave the site at all. "You ever drive the bumper cars at the state fair?"

"Yeah."

"Good. Knock him off the road. Carefully."

Rusty didn't even flinch. Instead, his face grew serious, his eyes locking in on Camden's retreating figure. "On it."

The man ran up the hill, chasing after his former site manager. Former, for sure, because there was no way Camden came back after that fight. As much as we'd hoped to get ahead of it, Camden was in free fall. He hadn't hit bottom yet. Hell, he couldn't even *see* the bottom yet. And maybe he never would—maybe he'd keep falling until he gave up and accepted the bottom didn't exist for him. That's what had happened with my dad—the man had never even attempted to clean himself up. He'd died just as much of a drunken mess as he'd lived. Camden deserved better, but he'd have to be willing to put the work in to get it.

I didn't have a lot of words for Alder when he came back my way, but there was one question I knew needed asking. "You okay?"

"I've known him since he was in diapers. Knew his parents. I can't believe it's come down to this." Alder took his moment, giving himself a few seconds to absorb the loss. Then the man did exactly what I knew he would—he yelled for Vol, getting right back down to business. And like the good man he was, Alder shook Vol's hand when the older man approached and gave him the respect he deserved. "I know you're not looking for the promotion, but I need you to be site lead for now."

Vol nodded once, likely expecting the job after Camden's fallout. "No problem, but I'd prefer it to be temporary."

"Understood. I'll start looking for others to take the spot right away. If you know of anyone you think might be ready, let me know."

"I'll make a list, though I'll tell you now, my son will be on it. That's not bias—I think he's ready for the role." Vol nodded to where Rusty had just disappeared into the forest. "He okay?"

Camden. Alder frowned deep at that question. "Says he's leaving Justice."

Vol sighed, the weight of those words dragging him down and making him look his age. "Not the best plan, but maybe getting away from the memories will give him some peace."

"Maybe. Why don't you let the guys break for twenty before we reset today's job? I think that'll help them get their heads on straight."

"This crew?" Vol grinned. "Ain't nothing going to straighten them out."

"Your son's on this crew."

"And he's the worst of the lot." Vol laughed and walked back toward the team of men waiting for him.

Alder groaned and cracked his neck, the smile he'd given the older logger falling fast. Businessman gone, soldier replacing him. "Gage?"

I knew the question coming before he asked it. "As of this morning, Pistol's still in Boulder."

Alder nodded, looking off into the woods. His entire body stiff and unrelenting. Pistol—his woman's stepbrother. The man who'd beaten her, who'd started the attacks on our town because of her, who had threatened to steal her away to his club so the men there could take things from her she wasn't willing to give. The man who had a real fucking short life expectancy for all those things.

I'd been looking into him for weeks, tracking him. Learning

everything about him from his job to his home life to where he bought his beer. Alder wanted to know it all, the Green Beret in him needing the information to devise a plan to take the guy out quietly. I'd have planted some C-4 and blown the shit out of the guy's house with him in it, but Alder wasn't that dramatic. He also had a girl at home who needed him to protect her—he couldn't do that from prison, so any plan we enacted had to be quiet, clean, and untraceable.

Alder had the patience of a saint, but even he had his limits. "I need to take him out."

No argument from me. "You ready to make that call yet?"

"No." He spat the word out, his frustration clear. "I've got two pieces to the puzzle left to place and a sheriff to keep out of the way."

I'd already handed over everything I'd learned about the guy —his habits, his schedules, who he dealt with, who he trusted. Whatever information Alder was waiting on had to be harder to get than that. The sheriff...that was a whole other story.

Alder sighed and rolled his shoulders, seeming to refocus on the here and now instead of what we all knew was coming. "You busy tonight?"

"Nope."

"Good. I need you to guard Main Street after hours."

He meant Katie's place—the only business open past six. That wouldn't be a hardship at all.

"Done."

"It's gumbo night."

Her late night. "No problem. I'll stay close to Katie."

"Good." He nodded, sliding a look my way that seemed almost devious. "You know she's the niece of the sheriff, right?"

Sheriff Baker—and yeah, I knew. "Bishop mentioned that once. Something I should know?"

"He's crooked as fuck, but he's blood to that girl. You make sure not to give him a reason to come digging around in town. He's a shark in the water—don't go throwing out chum."

In other words, don't fuck with Katie and leave her hurt. He had no worries there—if I ever got the girl in my bed, I had a feeling I'd never let her out.

"Won't be a problem."

Alder just nodded. "Good. Be safe out there. I'll be home but will keep my phone on me, so reach out if you need anything."

"Got it, boss." I couldn't let him walk away without saying one more thing. Because a real man admitted when he was wrong. "And hey, Alder."

"Yeah?"

"Sorry for all the shit I gave you these past three years. About Shye."

Alder held my gaze, a smile tugging at his mouth. "Every day now—every single one—is worth those three years, in case you were wondering."

I wasn't—I could tell that by the way he bounded into work every morning and how he rushed home every evening. Shye living with him had brought a joy to his life none of us could have expected, but we were all grateful for it. He deserved that happiness. Me? I might not deserve it, but I was going to reach for it anyway.

Chapter Four

KATIE

"Almost there." I stirred the mixture of flour and butter, watching the color turn darker. It'd been a long day—one where I had almost fallen into the weeds during the dinner rush —but I'd held everything together. I'd been at full staff tonight— two cooks in the kitchen, three waitresses on the floor—a first for me. The extra bodies had helped, and the men had obviously been satisfied with their meals. The plates had come back with hardly a scrap on them. And complaints? Not a one. Already, the diners seemed to be adjusting to the smaller dinner menu, though I'd promised them I'd have more options on the weekend. My plan for how to succeed with such a strange rush of diners every weekday might just work.

I stretched, my arm shaking as I stirred, trying to keep the thick mixture from burning. My back hurt from standing all day, and I couldn't stop thinking of my bed as the long hours wore down on me. But some soups needed to set up overnight, to give the flavors a chance to meld and deepen. I made a lot of soups after the dinner rush ended. Tomorrow, I'd serve gumbo as my lunch special. It was a favorite in town, and I knew I'd be too busy in the morning handing out to-go containers for the guys on their way into work to get it started in time for the melding. My gumbo absolutely needed to be made the night before.

As the roux turned a dark cardboard color, my mind wandered away from food. The color I wanted was darker, deeper. A fuller caramel sort of brown. Almost rich mahogany. Like some parts of Gage's hair. Not the darkness of it—that would mean a burned roux and having to start over on the whole process. No. I wanted the color of his highlights. That lighter, richer shade that women paid for and he probably came by naturally.

The color my roux finally turned just as my thoughts turned to wondering if his hair was that color all over.

"Not where your mind needs to go tonight," I singsonged, refocusing on the food. I added the mirepoix—bastardized with the addition of green pepper because gumbo required that flavor profile—and stirred. And stirred some more. And some more. Once the onions, carrots, and green pepper were fully coated and cooking down, I added way more garlic than I'd been taught—I couldn't help myself. It added such a spicy sort of sweetness to the dish. The kitchen smelled amazing already, and it would be even better tomorrow when I put the bread I'd started this morning in the oven. Gumbo and crusty, homemade bread? A perfect meal to satisfy even the hungriest logger in town. Even Gage. No special lunch for him—he loved my gumbo and bread.

As I continued making the gumbo, as the muscle memory kicked in and I lost myself in the repetitiveness of the movements, my mind settled and calmed. No stress, no fear, and none of the monsters that chased me through my dreams. I found peace when

I cooked. Food was easy. Food was balanced and fun and warmed your soul. There were no negative feelings in my kitchen, just the confidence born from years at a stove.

But thinking of confidence only reminded me of the times when I didn't feel the same way. Like with Gage anywhere near me? The exact opposite of confidence. I'd never been so nervous around another human being, and yet, I'd missed him tonight. He hadn't come in for dinner. Hadn't made me jump or scream. No matter how many times I'd looked up, expecting him to be standing silently off to the side, he hadn't been looming in the corner. I'd even missed his dog being in my kitchen.

"Quit thinking about Gage," I said, trying to wrangle control of my thoughts. I poured chicken stock into the pot and turned the burner down to simmer, finally ready to step away and let the heat do its job. I couldn't leave, though. There was always so much to do.

Next week, I'd be making crispy pan chicken with roasted vegetables, which meant I needed to make sure both my cast iron skillets were well seasoned and ready to use. I pulled them from the shelf where they lived, inspecting each for any sign of the seasoning layer flaking. One pan passed inspection, the other...

"Time to season you again, old girl."

I set the pan on a burner and turned the gas all the way up. Seasoning in the oven was better, but mine had been cool for hours. It'd take too long to warm it back up to the point I needed, so stovetop it was. As the pan heated, I grabbed the flaxseed oil and a potholder. It wouldn't save my hand from the pan once it reached the heat level I needed it to be at, but it'd protect me as I worked the oil over the dark surface.

Dark. Like Gage's eyes.

"You'll burn your hand off if you don't pay attention," I

whispered to myself. "And you should really get a radio so you stop talking to yourself."

Yeah. Thank goodness I was alone in the building.

I poured the oil into the pan, swirled it around to coat the bottom evenly, then put the pan back on the burner and let the heat do its job. The soup would cook for about an hour, and the pan would be ready to remove from the heat at about the same time. That left me at least sixty minutes of time to fill. As much as I dreaded the thought of tiring myself out more, I headed to the gym.

Well, okay—Justice didn't have a *gym*. What we did have was another storefront connected to mine by a set of double doors in the dining room and a hallway running along the back of the building. When my place had been a diner, the other space had been the smoking section. I hadn't wanted or needed the full space for my restaurant, so the room sat empty. At least, for a few weeks. Someone—probably one of the guys from the mill—had brought in exercise equipment recently, and a lot of people used the space to work out. Me included.

I changed out of my kitchen gear and into yoga pants and a tank top. My hair was already piled high on my head, and any makeup I might have put on had been melted off in the heat of a busy kitchen. Didn't matter, though—this late at night, the only person I usually saw was Camden, and he definitely didn't care what I looked like. He didn't care about much of anything anymore, it seemed. That worked out fine for me and my messy, no-makeup appearance. I needed sleep and some sun, but I wouldn't get that tonight. Instead, I'd get my nemesis.

The elliptical machine.

The only piece of equipment I used, and the only torture I put myself through. I wasn't stupid—being a chef meant eating, tasting, trying, sampling...whatever word you could use to describe adding calories to your diet one bite at a time, it worked. My body had always been a bit on the softer side—something my mother had made sure to point out at every turn—which meant working out was a must. Calories in, calories out, my mother had chanted when I'd been a child. As much as I may have wanted to forget those lessons, I couldn't. So I worked out.

And I hated every damn second of it.

I heard the sounds of someone lifting weights as I made my way through the back hallway. Most likely Camden, so I tucked in my earbuds. No sense trying to talk to him when he'd just grunt or ignore me. But when I turned the corner, when I actually made it into the workout space, I nearly dropped my phone. It wasn't Camden lifting weights—it was Gage. Shirtless, tattooed all over, wearing dark gray sweat pants that should not have looked so utterly sexy...Gage. Lifting weights. Shirtless.

Did I mention he had no shirt on?

God, that picture of him with his tattoos on full display would be burned into my brain for the rest of my life. Colors swirled from his wrists up his arms, filling in the planes of his chest as well. They even looped onto his neck, words and shadows and shapes drawing my eyes to the corded muscles there. And when he lifted the bar? When his arms extended and his muscles seemed to make the ink on his skin dance? I nearly moaned.

He looked like the cover model for some modern, edgy romance featuring a man who'd do anything for his girl. The hero to some perfectly coifed heroine who would get to touch and lick and enjoy every inch of that man for the rest of her life while being completely poised and pristine. Me? I was a hot mess. Literally. Kitchens got hot, and I sweated all day. This was so not fair.

I nearly ran away, nearly busted my butt back to the kitchen to hide and think about all that multicolored skin as I washed my face with the hand soap in the bathroom and tried to figure out a way to make myself look...well, less of a mess. Rex sold me out, though. The dog hurried over before I could escape, wagging his tail and catching Gage's attention. The hero of someone else's story pushed the bar back up into the holder, then sat up, looking all kinds of delicious as he turned my way.

Whoever that someone else was, his future heroine? I hated her with every fiber of my being.

I also had no chill left. "Oh. Hey. Sorry, I didn't mean to interrupt, but it's usually only Camden in here at night, and he doesn't pay any attention to anything anymore, so I don't think he minds that I come work out. Not that I work out like—" I waved a hand at him "—that. I just use the devil machine over there. Though, I usually do this in the morning before I start working because by the end of the night, I'm already super tired and sweaty and don't need to add to that. I know it's not my normal schedule. Maybe I should just—"

"It's late," Gage said, watching me. Resting his elbows on his thick, thick thighs and leaning forward. Abs, abs, and more abs... that was all I could see. Gage Shepherd was the biggest distraction in my world.

I had to swallow hard before I could speak again. "That's what I was saying."

"No, you were telling me when you usually come in here." He stood, rising to his feet like some sort of superhero. Like Aquaman in that movie trailer that made all the girls scream. Made them all wet, too. And when he grabbed a towel? When he wiped that lucky, lucky terry cloth down the muscles of his chest and neck? I might have died just a little.

He made words so hard.

"I...yeah. That."

The slow smile that spread across his face might as well have been a stroke of his finger across my clit for how much it made me shiver. "What are you doing here so late?"

I wanted to answer in a sentence, I really did, but the man had his hands on his waistband and was tugging the elastic away from his skin to mop up the sweat dripping down his—fuck, how could I be expected to count—eight-pack abs? Eight. And he had that V. Every woman knows that V—the muscles that dipped down along a guy's hip bones and made us go stupid. He had that V, and it accomplished its job with me just fine. I had no words...save one.

"Gumbo."

He nodded, moving around the weight bench to the side with the arm support thing. Technical term.

"You like it to set up overnight."

"That's right. And I usually work out in the mornings, but I was running late today, so I figured I could hop on the elliptical while the gumbo simmered. I didn't mean to interrupt you."

The intense look he sent my way practically melted me. "You didn't interrupt anything. Go ahead."

I wanted to move, I really did, but he kept those dark eyes on me as he raised a water bottle to his mouth. As his bicep flexed and he licked his lips. As he chugged that cool liquid down.

Jesus, I was about to come from watching a man take a drink of water.

"I'll just..." I pointed toward the elliptical and shoved my earbud back in. I needed an escape, a reason to stop staring, and making my muscles hurt on that blasted machine was about as good of an excuse as any.

But I hadn't thought of the logistics of getting *on* the elliptical, or the positioning of all the equipment. I had to turn my back on Gage, had to climb up onto the foot pedals of a machine taller than I was. Whoever designed this demon had obviously not intended it for people as short as me. I also had to use my legs to make the pedals move to get the beast turned on. That took strength and coordination, of which I had very little. I did it, though—of course, I nearly fell forward when the machine kicked on and the pedals moved more freely.

Smooth, Katie. Real smooth.

But hey, I had two slices of bread to work off. And a piece of cobbler. And...a few other things I'd sampled. I needed this workout, so I set the display to see my strides per minute, upped the resistance to a respectable level four, and got to it.

Two minutes in, and I knew even the burn of going backward without hands wouldn't work to clear my head, though. All I could think about was Gage. Was he lifting again? Was he looking at me, staring at my ass as I worked out? Was my ass good enough to attract his attention? Did I want it to be? I'd look at his ass, for sure, especially tonight. What was it with men in sweat pants? Something about the casualness of it, maybe. Or the way they couldn't hide much underneath. Were they the leggings of the male wardrobe? Comfy and casual, but deep down, men knew they hugged their ass and hips just right. Or the yoga pants of his clothing choices—totally appropriate for working out, but he ended up wearing them more often simply because they were comfy. I could almost see a future with Gage—me in my yoga pants, him in his sweat pants. I'd make him a nice bowl of soup with some good bread, and we'd end up on the couch doing horribly naughty things under the yoga pants and sweats.

Things I needed to stop thinking about before I fell off the cursed machine.

Dating was *not* on my radar. I had a business to build and a life to start all over again after leaving Denver behind in such a rush. All with no support system—my mother had passed away a few years back, and the only other relative I had was her brother, who I had absolutely no interest in talking to ever again. I had the Kennards and the men they employed backing me up because I was from Justice—that was all. I couldn't risk my place with them.

And Gage...he likely wasn't interested in me like that anyway. How could he be? I word-vomited all over him every time I saw him. And he was always so cool, so controlled. Calm. I was anything but. Pretty much always had been.

I was either too much or not enough for a man like Gage Shepherd.

I pushed a little harder, focusing on the burn building in my thighs and trying hard to psychically will the calories I'd ingested to burn away. Calories in, calories out.

Ugh. *Thanks, Mom.*

For all her faults and all her craziness, I missed her. She'd been an aerobicizing junkie back in the days of Suzanne Somers commercials and Thighmasters. Always working out, always watching what she ate. Constantly fighting those ten pounds she was convinced were somehow holding her back from everything good in life. I'd watched her try every fad diet and health program out there. And I'd hated it.

I'd hated the boxed dinners and freezer meals purchased from some diet company promising a better life if you only ate their stuff.

I'd hated the fake food flavorings added to things because the real stuff would add to the calorie count.

I'd hated the tracking and weighing and constant need to trim off just a little more.

I'd hated thinking that eating all that crap had caused her colon cancer, and that was why I'd become a chef, why I'd taken so many courses on nutrition and dietary needs. I'd developed the opinion that food should be food—not chemicals pretending to be food. If I plated something, I wanted to be able to tell the diner exactly what was in it and why, without either of us needing a chemical engineering degree.

And even though I couldn't take care of my mom anymore, I could still cook. I could take care of the little town where I'd grown up, the only place I felt safe anymore. I could feed the people I cared about real food without obsessing over every single calorie in a dish.

My mother would have hated seeing the amount of butter in my restaurant, but I didn't care. Butter was natural and real. And good. Butter was always good.

I was thinking about grabbing some of the leftover bread from the day—what I'd been planning to make bread pudding with—and slathering it with butter as a post-workout snack when the machine beeped at me. Calories spent goal achieved—workout over. Thank the stars.

I hopped off the demon I'd officially tamed and grabbed my towel, wiping the sweat from the back of my neck as I took a drink of my water. Definitely bread and butter. And maybe some cheese. Cheese was good too, though it deserved wine. If I waited until I got home, I could have all of it...and some fruit to cut the heaviness of the bread and butter. Grapes and apples, maybe. A boring night alone had never sounded so good.

But as I turned around, I found Gage sitting on the weight bench, eating a store-bought granola bar out of a shiny package. My words came unbidden, something left over from thinking about my mom and her diets. About the sickness that had taken her away from me.

"I can make you something way better than that."

Eyebrows up, Gage glanced down at the bar in his hand and slowly lowered it. Shit. I hadn't meant to food-shame him.

"I just mean, that's fake food. They combine all of these

chemicals to imitate the flavor and texture of food, but it's not really food, you know? But you can make them with real food. Or I can. Nuts and nut butters for protein, oats to fill you up, dates for sweetness. They'd be much better for you. Not that you're not doing fine on your own. I mean, you look fine. Not fine like *fine* but like...healthy. You look healthy." Did I just tell him he wasn't fine? Because that was the biggest goddamned lie of my life. My internal groan would have shattered a window or two, it was so loud. Time to retreat. "I should go check on my gumbo."

"I hate these things."

I stopped, frozen halfway through a step to walk out the door. "What?"

"These bars. They're Bishop's. I hate them."

"Then why are you eating one?"

He shrugged, one ink-covered, massive shoulder rising and lowering in a smooth sort of arc. "Knew I needed to work out and didn't have anything else to bring with me."

Well, now I felt like a jerk. He probably didn't have time to cook, what with working and guarding the town. Which was probably what he was doing in the gym so late—guarding me, the only person dumb enough to work past sunset when the town had already been attacked by the Soul Suckers. My opinion of myself needed clarification—I was not just a jerk, but a *huge* jerk.

"I'm sorry, I didn't mean to—"

"Katie?"

"Yeah?"

"You ever make some of those bars you talked about, I'd love to try them."

Flutters. I felt them all over at the tone in his voice and the way he looked at me when he said that. "Really?"

"Yes."

"Okay. Great." I clapped my hands together, my grin

unstoppable. "I'll make some. Not tonight because I've got gumbo going and I've already kept you here late enough, plus I need to get up early to try a new bread recipe. Not sure it's going to work out. It requires kneading, and I hate kneading bread."

Gage rose to his feet, moving closer. Stealing all the oxygen from the air around us. "How do you make bread without kneading it?"

He...expected me to think when he stood close enough to touch? "Time. It works magic. You give the dough enough time, and the yeast will do the job for you."

Oh god. He was so close, and he smelled so good. Like everything tasty all thrown together into the most perfect combination known to man. Like something I wanted in my mouth.

Speaking of mouths, his was only a few inches from mine as he said, "What if you're tired of waiting?"

Why are we waiting?

"I mean...there are faster ways," I said, trying hard to concentrate on bread. "I have an industrial mixer, so I can mix anything. The machine does most of the work, but then I have to take the dough and let it rest, punch it down, all that stuff. Eventually, I have to knead at least a little bit, but given enough time, the yeast really handles—"

"Katie."

I couldn't breathe, he was so close. Looking at me. Devouring me with his eyes. "Yeah?"

He stepped even closer, and my heart dive-bombed into my stomach. "I love how excited you get about food."

And then his lips were on mine, and all thoughts about food or the restaurant or anything other than the warmth of his lips, the slickness of his tongue, and the feel of his beard against my face flew right out the window.

Chapter Five

GAGE

I don't know what made me kiss her. Okay, I totally knew. That ass. I'd been sitting on the weight bench watching her on that damned machine for twenty minutes trying to figure out if I had enough blood in the rest of my body to be able to move. To get up, maybe walk to the little restroom in the back, and jack off. To do something other than stare at the way her ass looked in those tight, black...were they pants? No way could those be pants. If she wore those out of her house on a regular basis, I'd have noticed. I'd have chased her down and made her cover up until I could get her alone and enjoy them. Because I definitely enjoyed them. So did my cock. I'd never been so damn hard.

So I kissed her.

Soft and plump, her lips met mine, opening for me as I stole a taste of her. Too damn sweet for words, this girl. I wanted to devour her. Wanted to lick every inch of her, see how she tasted all over. Wanted to trace my name on her thighs with my tongue as I gripped that ass tight. Wanted to get my mouth on her cunt and drink down every drop as I made her scream my name.

I wanted everything.

I slicked my tongue against hers and grabbed her ass, the one that had been torturing me in those pants. The one causing me to hate Camden for getting to see it in workout pants for the last few weeks as he took morning guard duty on Main Street. Had he even noticed how that ass jiggled when she moved? How the muscles of her thighs bunched and strained, pushing that perfect, round peach up even higher? Probably not—and thank fuck for that. If it'd been any other guy, they'd have been all over Katie's ass just like I was. And then I would have had to kill them.

Hell, it was my ass now. Claim made. I squeezed Katie's perfect cheeks hard, lifting, picking her up easy. Those thighs I wanted to crawl between opened and spread for me, those legs wrapping around my waist. All the while, I kept kissing her— kept sucking on her lips and tangling my tongue with hers. Kept doing whatever I needed to so she'd keep her hands locked in my hair, keep her body open and warm against mine. Keep letting me grip that heart-stopping ass.

Seriously, how would I ever get enough?

"Gage," she gasped when I pressed her to the wall. I grunted, rocking my hips into hers as I nibbled and licked down her neck. Still sweet, this girl. Still tugging on me as if needing more. She would be the death of me for sure if she kept that up.

I ran my hands down her legs to her knees and back up, gripping her thighs tight as I went. Finally getting a feel of her. Katie had curves for days—thick thighs that made you want to spread them and use one as a pillow as you ate her, wide hips meant to sway and bounce on your cock, an ass that never quit, and tits made for gripping, squeezing, and fucking. So bitable, this girl. So soft—the exact opposite of me—and I loved every fucking inch.

I rolled my hips against hers, harder this time, staring down at her as her eyes popped open. As her jaw dropped and she moaned in a way that made me want to come in my pants like a goddamned teenager.

"So fucking beautiful." I yanked her closer, keeping our bodies tightly together. I couldn't say much else. If I did, if I opened my mouth one more time, everything I thought about her would spill out. Like how I wanted to rip those pants off her body so I could suck on her little clit. How I loved the way her tits bounced and couldn't wait to lay her down and get my hands on them. Like how if I didn't get to see her come, I might lose my goddamned mind.

I couldn't say all that, so I kissed her again instead.

Katie opened right away for me, groaning as I tasted that sweet mouth once more. Hands tightening in my hair as I thrust against her. Fabric. All that was between my cock and her hot pussy were a couple of layers of fabric. I wanted them gone, wanted to bury myself deep, to ease the ache she'd been causing in my balls since the second I'd seen her. I wanted all of her. And if the heat I felt coming from her—the way she held me tight and rocked her body against mine—was any indication, she wanted me, too.

I had to tell her. Needed to.

"Fuck, Katie. So hot. Your pussy is so fucking hot against me. You're ready for my cock, aren't you, princess?"

I growled as she tilted her hips, as she groaned and arched and moved against me. I could *feel* her—those pants she wore hid nothing from me, and with the way she angled her hips, my cock laid right against her entrance, practically hugged by her pussy. Fuck, the pants had to be pulled so tight to let me be almost inside her, had to stretch and give to conform to her body like that. When she was mine, when I got to fuck that sweet pussy every day, I'd make sure she only wore pants like these around me. I mean, I'd rather have her naked, but these were fun.

"I'm going to come," she said, and I surged forward. Wanting that so badly. To see her give herself up to what I did to her body. "Gage, please. I'm so close."

Filter...destroyed.

"Jesus, princess. I'm going to lick you so long and deep the next time I get you alone. Going to kiss every inch of this body, including that sweet pussy. You'd like that, wouldn't you? Like me to own your little clit with my mouth. Like me to suck up every drop and beg for more. I will, Katie. I'll beg for you like it's my damn job."

She curled into me as I kept thrusting against her, as I gripped her ass tight and let my fingers dig deep to pull her open for me. As I—

Heard Rex growl.

I froze, listening, every sense I had no longer on Katie. She wiggled and moaned, but I couldn't move. Couldn't speak. I'd missed something, but Rex hadn't. He stared at the door to Katie's restaurant, ears up and body stiff. And then he growled again.

Fuck. We had company.

And Katie didn't know. "Why are you—"

I shushed her as Rex growled louder, straining my ears to hear anything. Anything at all other than our own harsh breaths. Katie stiffened in my arms, a sure sign I'd just fucked up in her mind.

"Get off me."

Yup. Big-time fucked up. But she couldn't have seen Rex, and she most likely hadn't heard anything yet. I really didn't want to scare her, so I pressed into her body a little harder, pinned her in place a little more securely. Covering her just in case someone rushed the door.

And then I leaned in to whisper in her ear. "Katie—"

"I'm not a child. You don't get to shush—"

I clamped my hand over her mouth, knowing I wasn't making things better. Trying hard to control my need to protect her and her need to know what the fuck was happening.

Her need won out over mine. "Someone's next door."

She blinked as I leaned back, those wide, hazel eyes darting to the door behind me before meeting mine once more.

I couldn't stand to see her scared.

"I need to check on the restaurant, see who's over there. There's a closet on the other side of the bathroom in the back corner here. You got your phone?" I wanted to curse when she shook her head in the negative. "Grab mine out of my bag. The passcode is 5284. Text Alder for backup."

I let her legs down, backing away even though it was the last thing I wanted to do. Katie didn't follow my whispered instructions. Instead, she stood there, looking so small and scared. Staring at me as if she might never see me again. Tough chance on that happening. She was mine now, and I'd make damn sure to come back to her no matter what. So I put my finger against her mouth and quietly shushed her again, a reminder to stay silent once she got in the closet. She grabbed my hand and tugged me closer, rising on the balls of her feet to place the sweetest, softest kiss of my life on me.

"Be careful," she breathed against my lips.

I ran my hand over her ass, dropping down to nuzzle her neck as I whispered, "I'm more worried about you. Phone, 5284, Alder, and hide. Now."

She stared at me for another moment, looking almost lost, breaking my heart with every passing second. But there was nothing I could do—she needed to hide, and I needed to make sure she stayed safe.

When she finally walked away, moving to grab my phone as I'd asked her to do, I breathed a little easier. She'd be okay locked back there. At least she had a better shot just in case the fuckers at the restaurant decided to come through that door. Before she was out of my sight, though, I gave Rex the hand signal to follow her, making sure they were locked up tight together so I wouldn't be distracted. Then I dove into action.

Just in time, too, because the noises next door moved closer with every minute.

I snagged the gun I'd hidden under the weight bench and crept to the door connecting this room to the dining room at The Baker's Cottage. French doors—flimsy wood, no lock, and way too much fucking glass—were all that stood between me and whatever was on the other side. I moved the thin, white curtain covering the doors enough to peek out. Three men moved through the shadows at Katie's place. Shit. Three to one with me having such an important target to guard were not odds I wanted to have to take. I'd have given anything to have Bishop with me, but the fucker was in Vegas with Anabeth again, which meant I was on my own. Just me, three targets to take down, and the woman I'd been having wet dreams about for months hiding out in a flimsy closet without a lock on the door. What could possibly go wrong?

I ran through my options as fast as I could—full-out attack was no good. I didn't have a silencer on my gun, so if I ended up having to shoot, the whole damn area would know it. Slipping out the back door or even onto the street sucked because I had no idea if they had more men waiting for us. They'd obviously come to the restaurant looking for someone, which meant they probably knew Katie would be here and likely alone. That pissed me the fuck off. The only way they'd know that was if our surveillance was off and they'd been sneaking into town—not a likely option considering how tight Alder'd been running the guards—or if they had insider info. Someone local slipping them details about the residents. Someone we wouldn't suspect.

Much more likely, and much more infuriating.

The noises on the other side of the door suddenly got louder—a voice added to the mix of bumps and footsteps.

"Where's the girl?"

"Don't know. Baker said she'd be here past nine. Something about cooking."

Baker. Katie Baker. Also Sheriff Baker. Her uncle. Fuck me, the guy was as crooked as they came in law enforcement, but would he really sell out his own blood? Looked like it.

"Well, Baker was wrong," the first guy said, obviously moving closer to the doors.

"There's food on the stove in the kitchen. Something cooking in a big pot and a pan on a lit burner."

Shit. No way would someone leave food cooking and not be close, and those fuckers likely knew that. I figured I had about sixty seconds to get Katie out of here, which wasn't even close to enough time.

"Find her." Guy One sounded pissed. "The bitch has to be around here somewhere. Pistol wants leverage, so we're not leaving without her."

Pistol, which meant the Soul Suckers. And Katie's uncle, Sheriff Baker. We'd known they were in bed together, but this was different. This was confirmation that the county sheriff was working with the motorcycle gang attacking our town.

It also meant Sheriff Baker had sold out his niece to a band of lawless thugs, something I couldn't tell her. Not yet. Not until I had her safely tucked away where he couldn't get to her.

But once I had her secured? I hoped—I actually hoped—both men showed up in town, because there would be a reckoning coming their way. And if they didn't? If they stayed away like the cowards I knew them to be?

We'd hunt them down and drag their sorry asses right back to Main Street.

And then neither man would make it out of Justice alive.

Chapter Six

KATIE

I'd never been afraid of the dark as a child. Anything bad that had happened to me in the dark had occurred as an adult. I still wasn't afraid of the blackness, though I had to admit, standing in the closet alone, save for Rex at my feet, made me uncomfortable. Add in the fact that I was in said closet because bad guys had broken in to my restaurant? That feeling jumped right up there to terrified.

I clutched Gage's phone in my hands, wishing it would buzz. I'd texted Alder as Gage had told me to but hadn't gotten a response. Alder would respond...wouldn't he? At least to let us know he was on his way or that he'd gotten the message? I hadn't sent him my name—just a note that men were in the restaurant and Gage needed backup. Exactly what Gage had told me. Why wasn't Alder texting back?

But all thoughts of the phone and Alder disappeared when the door suddenly opened and a big, warm body pressed against mine before the darkness blanketed me again. A hand slipped over my mouth before I could scream, another around my waist as the person pulled me closer. Close enough to get a good, long feel of him.

Gage.

My panic melted away, leaving me buzzing and on edge. Gage was back. With me in the dark. That had to be a good thing, right?

Gage curled his body over mine, bringing his face closer as the palm over my mouth moved to the back of my neck. As he held me against him with rough hands and stiff muscles. Tense. The man was so damn tense.

Maybe not a good thing after all.

"Three men at least," he whispered, his breath warm on my ear. His beard brushing against my skin in an almost tickling sort of way. "They're looking for you, so we have to go right now. Did you text Alder?"

I nodded, shaking as I clung to his bicep with one hand, his phone still in my other. His presence, his closeness, almost calmed me. Not quite, though, because I still trembled, unable not to. Unable to push down the fear digging holes through my soul. *They're looking for you.* But...why? That didn't make sense.

Gage kissed my cheek—so soft and simple—before cupping my face in his big hands. "I'll get you out, okay, princess? I promise. Just do whatever I say."

I nodded, taking a deep breath when he let me go so he could grab my hand. The startled jerk he gave at finding his phone in the way pulled me up short. Him, too, though he didn't take it from me.

"Hang on to that," he said, his voice still so very quiet.

I tried to match that whispered tone. "I don't have pockets."

He took the device from my hand, his skin rough but his

touch gentle. I still couldn't see, but I could feel as he raised his arms up. Not high—chest height. My chest height.

I nearly whimpered when he grabbed the neckline of my shirt and tugged... To tuck the phone inside my bra.

"What's the code?" he asked, his voice deep, his hand still resting against my breast. His body rigid against mine.

But I remembered. "5284."

"Good job, princess. If we get separated, if anything happens to me, you call for help. Alder, Deacon, Finn, Bishop—doesn't matter. I go down, you call everyone in my contacts until someone answers, okay?"

"Gage—"

"Promise me."

I nodded, tears welling fast and hot as the reality that we were really about to risk our lives to run washed over me. I didn't want anything to happen to him. I didn't want anything to happen to either of us, but I also had no control over what was going on. All I could do was follow his directions and hope he could get us out of danger. He had to be able to—he'd been a Navy SEAL, one of the most dangerous types of military professionals on the planet. He knew what he was doing. The likelihood of screwing up our escape and getting us killed fell on me.

"There's a ladder for roof access at the far end of the back hallway. It's the safest bet for now. Let's go." Gage pulled me behind him, both of us creeping out of the closet and toward the back hallway. The one that connected this space to my restaurant. Where the bad guys were. If this had been a cartoon, I would have gulped. Instead, I gripped Gage's hand tighter and made sure Rex kept up with us. If the man was going to risk his life to watch over me, the least I could do in return was to watch over his dog.

I didn't get the chance to watch for long.

Before we could make it through the dimly lit hallway to the ladder that led to the roof, a huge boom sounded, and the doors to the restaurant kitchen exploded. I screamed and ducked, falling sideways as Gage shoved me into a wall and covered me with his body. Rex was barking at something ahead of us, the sound sharp and mean. Distracting. At least, until Gage grabbed my face.

"Up," he said, his eyes darker than I'd ever seen them. "Get up on the roof. Now."

He pulled me off the floor by my arm and shoved me toward the ladder as three men burst through my destroyed kitchen doors. Gage moved fast, faster than I thought possible, raising his arms straight out and holding...

Oh my god, a gun.

I hadn't noticed it, hadn't seen or felt it, but there it was. Gripped tight in his hands—one clutching the grip, the other underneath—the metal so dark, it practically absorbed the light, so deadly it stole my breath. For about a half of a second, which was exactly how long it took for Gage to pull the trigger.

One shot. That was all it took for the first man to drop. The one with the shotgun, which must have been the boom that splintered the kitchen doors. Not a bomb—a gun. Just as deadly in my mind. Just as scary. Scary enough to make me pause, make me look over the men running straight at Gage. Make me not take those first few steps up the ladder.

Such a mistake.

As one man slammed into Gage, charging the bigger man like a bull and making him drop his gun, the other grabbed me around the waist and pulled me off my feet. Seconds. I'd lasted seconds before I'd screwed things up.

"Been looking for you, chef."

The man's breath reeked of alcohol and onions, and his arms felt like steel bands wrapped around me. I couldn't fight. Couldn't escape. Gage and Rex were both battling their own assailant, one's fists flying and the other's teeth bared. I couldn't even scream for them before the guy who held me bent down to grab Gage's gun from the floor then raced into the kitchen. Still carrying me, carting me off as if I weighed absolutely nothing. And maybe to him, I didn't. Like Gage, he towered over me by at least a foot, and his arms bulged with muscles. Strong. Stronger than Gage, I doubted, but enough to take care of me without breaking a sweat. I was so screwed.

The man finally set me down and shoved me into my cooking area, a galley-like space with a prep counter on one side, the pass-through for order pickup on the other, and the stove, flat top, and fryer between the two. I lived in that space, owned it, knew every inch of it. He'd just dropped me into my domain, but I had to figure out how to get out of it alive.

As the sounds of the battle in the back hallway continued, the guy pulled a phone from his pocket and made a call. The man wore a black leather vest with the Soul Suckers colors on the back and a patch on the front that read Rock. His dark hair hung long and greasy, a scar on his chin the only part of him not pale. I absorbed every detail I could just in case I needed to tell someone—Gage, Alder, the police. That was something I could control, something I could do to help. Pay attention to the details.

At least until a voice came over the phone. "Status?"

Rock glanced my way as he paced, his light blue eyes hard and unreadable. "Got her, but the bearded guy took out Edge."

"You eliminate the target?"

"Judas is working on it now. Not sure he's going to win this one."

"Pistol just wants the girl, so get her out."

Rock stopped, his shoulders stiff and his back straight. "Leave Judas?"

"If he can't take down one scraggly mountain man, that's on him. Get the girl back here."

"I'm on it." Rock disconnected the call, looking me up and down before raising his arm. Pointing Gage's gun in my face with a sadistic sort of grin. "Looks like you're with me, chef."

The hell I was. I stepped away, backing into the stove. The very hot stove where the gumbo still simmered and the cast iron pan gave off enough heat to make me flinch. Every self-defense class I'd ever taken had instilled the same basic lesson—never let an attacker take you anywhere. Things would only get worse if they did, so you had to stand your ground where the attacker first came for you. I was in my kitchen, in my space, knowing every niche and crevice and tool within reach. If he walked me out of this building, I wouldn't know anything, wouldn't have the same advantages as I did right then.

This would be the place I'd make my stand. It might also end up being the place I died, but at least I'd go down on my terms.

Before I could even begin to think of a plan of attack, the broken doors slammed open, Gage and the other guy, Judas, crashing through them as they continued to fight. Blood flew and dripped, but I couldn't tell whose. I didn't have time to because Rock spun to watch, taking his attention off of me. How could he not? Two men throwing punches and grunting as they slammed each other into walls and tables plus Rex barking and growling like a beast set loose, biting Judas wherever he could reach and doing his best to protect his master. How could anyone tear their eyes away from such a show? At least, that was what I hoped—that Rock would keep watching them, giving me a chance to do something to help Gage.

The idea formed quickly, thoughts flying through my head as Rock tore his eyes away from the battle and returned his attention to me. As he glowered my way and took a step closer.

As he dropped his arm, the gun still in his hand, and reached as if to grab me again.

A move he'd soon regret.

In the world of cooking—whether home cooks or professional ones—burns were common. Normal enough that chefs tended to grow almost resistant to heat. Almost. Because even with the towel that I quickly snagged off the prep counter hook, I knew this was going to hurt. I could only hope I had the strength to ignore the instincts that would tell me not to do what I needed to. That I could force my body to accept the pain I was about to put it through.

Temporary. It's all temporary.

I caught Gage's eyes just before I moved, looked right into those inky depths as he wrapped an arm around the neck of Judas and pulled the man against him. I knew what was coming, but it didn't matter. Nothing mattered. Rock had Gage's gun, and even if Gage took Judas down, Rock would shoot him. And Rex. And then he'd drag me out of the restaurant, and god only knew what would happen to me.

Actually, I knew what would happen. At least, part of it. I'd fought my way out of a shitty situation once before. I could do it again. The stakes were just a little higher, and this was going to be a little more painful. But burns healed. Bones healed. A gunshot wound to the head didn't.

I could do this. I had to.

The world slowed, giving me time to see everything play out. To notice how Gage grimaced and pulled against Judas, how the man's head jerked to the side in the most unnatural of ways. How Rock raised the gun again, pointing it at Gage's face. Aiming. No way could Gage cross the kitchen before Rock shot, no way could he get himself out of the line of fire. I knew that with a certainty I couldn't have explained, so I did the only thing I could think of.

What I needed to. I wrapped the towel around my hand. And I chanted in my head as I reached behind me.

Don't let go. Don't let go. Don't let go. I grabbed the handle of the cast iron skillet, chanting louder than the instincts telling me to let go of the thing hurting me. Adding my other hand for leverage and strength. Hefting the heavy, hot thing without screaming. I swung that pan as if my life depended on it. Because it did. So did Gage's.

The towel slipped, my palm hitting metal as the heavy pan struck Rock in the face. And in that moment, as fire practically dripped down my hand and burned its way up my arm, I had no idea whose screams were louder—Rock's or mine.

"Katie." Gage pushed me back, knocking the pan from my hands and grabbing me by the shoulders. I couldn't see past my tears, couldn't hear anything but the rush of blood through my head as the pain dug its claws into my palm and tore out every nerve and muscle. But then Gage cupped my face again, his hands rough on my skin but his gaze boring into mine. His black eyes right in front of me.

"What did you do?" he asked, looking so worried. So scared. He'd shot a man in front of me, had likely just killed a second by breaking his neck. He'd done both without an ounce of apprehension. But this? His face as he held me while I cried and shook and cradled my injured hand? I'd never seen him so upset.

"He was going to shoot you."

The doors to the dining room whooshed open, closing almost immediately with a softer sort of sound I knew well. Someone had just left the kitchen. Rock was gone.

And he likely still had Gage's weapon. "You have to go after him."

The clench of his jaw gave away Gage's turmoil. "No. I have to get you out of here."

"Gage, he knows you killed those other men. He has your gun. That has to be some sort of nasty leverage to a group like the Soul Suckers."

"I'll deal with it. Let's go."

"Gage—"

He tugged me closer, eyes locked on mine. Intense and almost brutal as he said, "You are more important than the blowback coming my way. I need you safe before I deal with this, and you're not safe here."

I nodded, unable to speak again. Not that I needed to. He was in charge, and I was in pain. I could give up control to him, could trust him to do what was right while I dealt with the shock of my injury. Everything hurt. Everything burned. And with the way my palm looked—red skin, flesh torn away, blisters already forming—I knew the pain would only get worse.

Gage ushered me out of the kitchen, keeping himself between me and the dead guy on the floor as he directed me through the back hallway. A pool of blood had spread from the wounds on the first man down—the one who'd been aiming a shotgun at us before Gage shot him. The man Rock had called Edge.

The first person I'd ever seen die, and yet not the last.

Those men had come for me—had been sent to Justice to kidnap me. I had no idea why. I was nobody—a nothing chef in an even more nothing town. How could I possibly be worth so much death? It didn't make sense.

Gage didn't seem interested in trying to figure out the why of the situation, though. Not right then at least. He kept us moving, pausing only long enough to peek into the alley before throwing the door open and rushing outside.

Right into the path of another man with a gun.

"Jesus, son." Alder Kennard slowly dropped his weapon.

"Can't say I expected you to come bursting out the back door like that. If the Soul Suckers had staked out—"

"Katie's hurt," Gage interrupted, pushing me toward the truck parked at the far end of the alley. "She needs a doctor."

Deacon Manns, owner of the only bar in the area and best friend to Alder, came running from the other end, a large, scary-looking rifle sort of gun in his hands. "What's the situation?"

Gage never stopped moving. "Three men came for Katie. Two dead inside, one with a gunshot wound to the head, the other with a snapped neck. Third guy took off before I could take him down."

"Fuck," Alder spat, the word practically hissing through his lips. "And Katie?"

"Burned the hell out of her hand and the third guy's face. You'll know him coming for sure."

"Potential blowback?"

Gage paused, leaving a small moment of silence. A tiny delay I doubted Alder recognized, but one I caught. "Third guy—"

"Rock," I said, swallowing hard as the pain I fought made my voice tight and small. "The patch on his vest said Rock. Gunshot wound is Edge and broken neck is Judas."

Gage stared down at me, one side of his lips curling up a fraction. "Rock saw me take down the other two, and he has my gun."

"Motherfucker," Deacon said. "What now?"

"We get Katie medical care," Alder said, following us all the way to the truck and opening the passenger door so Gage could help me inside. "You think they'll come back for her?"

Gage's answer came hard and fast, his voice dangerous enough to send ice shooting up my spine. "Absolutely."

"Then we get her out of town. Tonight."

Gage spun on Alder, keeping one hand on my thigh as if

needing to feel me. To know I was right there with him. A touch I was thankful for.

"Not without me."

"You disappearing will bring more heat from the sheriff," Alder said, an inscrutable expression on his face. "We need to handle the witness and the stolen gun, but until then, you need to keep up the appearance that nothing is wrong. If you go running, you look guilty."

But Gage wasn't having that. "Katie can't stay in town."

"She can still go—I'll send Deacon with her. But you have to stay."

Just the thought, the idea of being separated from Gage, had my heart jumping in my chest. Thankfully, Gage seemed to understand that. He gripped my thigh tighter, shaking his head as he growled out a, "Not good enough."

"You willing to risk it? Because you already said they'd come for her." Alder glanced at me before cocking his head. "She has to be protected."

"I'll handle it."

And he would. I knew it. Trusted it.

Alder didn't seem convinced. "She'll need twenty-four-hour guards."

Strong and determined, Gage didn't even hesitate. "I'll handle that too."

Alder stood waiting, his face drawn as he appeared to think over Gage's arguments. "Katie?"

I met his steely blue eyes straight on. "Yeah?"

"You have an opinion on this?"

I set the back of my aching hand on Gage's where it still gripped my thigh. Perhaps needing to feel him as much as he needed to feel me. "I'm staying with Gage."

If my answer surprised the eldest Kennard, he didn't show it.

"Okay then." Alder's hard gaze moved to Gage, a fury blazing there that I'd never seen. "But this is on you. Make sure you've got yourself set up, and have a plan ready in case the heat gets to be too much."

"Yes, sir." With one last squeeze, Gage let me go, shutting the door before running around the front to the driver's side. He hopped into the truck with animalistic grace, practically sliding into place behind the wheel. "Where do I go, Deacon?"

"It's a burn, right?" Deacon asked, coming to stand in the open door. "Hit up the emergency room over in Crystal Falls. It's small, but they won't question anything too much."

"Got it." Gage started the engine. "And the restaurant?"

"I've got your back on cleanup."

"Good. Because if the sheriff pins this on me..."

He trailed off, glancing my way with an almost violent look on his face. I understood the unsaid. If they pinned those murders on him, if they came to take him to jail, my protector would be gone.

And I'd be as good as dead.

I scooted closer to Gage, resting my left hand on his thigh and squeezing tight, just as he'd gripped mine earlier. Offering what support I could give him while taking the comfort I needed. Gage looked down at me, dark eyes giving nothing away. But I knew. I understood his worries, and they matched my own.

"Hey, Deacon." I didn't risk breaking eye contact with my brave man, didn't let go of him either. "Don't fuck this up."

Deacon snorted a laugh. "Jesus, son. You've got your hands full with this one."

Gage's half smile brought out one of my own, and he shook his head. "You don't need to tell *me* that. I've already figured it out." He moved as if to put the truck in gear, finally dragging his gaze away from me and back to Deacon. "Take Rex with you."

Jesus, Rex. I hadn't even looked for him since the kitchen, but I did then, spotting him with ease. The dog sat at Alder's feet, watching us. Somehow looking regal in all his fuzziness. No longer baring his teeth or attacking anyone. Such a smart, brave dog...when I got back into my kitchen, I was totally making him a steak.

Deacon knocked his fist against the side of the door. "No problem. I'll bring him back to you tomorrow."

Without warning, I shivered violently, the cold washing over me so fast, the waves of it hurt more than just my hand. My entire body felt that ache. Through chattering teeth, I whispered, "Gage."

"Gotta go," Gage said. Deacon nodded and stepped away from the truck just before Gage slammed the door, and then we were moving. Speeding down the alley and out onto Main Street at a rate well over the legal limit. Once on the highway heading out of town, Gage pulled me closer into his side. Laying his heavy arm over my shoulders and giving me a place to rest my head. "I've got you."

Yeah, he did. Still... "I'm cold."

"Just stay awake, okay?"

"I'll try."

He was silent for a long time. But then...

"You were amazing back there."

"I don't feel amazing." I snuggled closer. "You saved me."

"I got you hurt."

"You killed people." Another silence, but this time, I broke it. "Thank you."

"For killing people?"

"For caring enough to be willing to do that." I groaned as a wave of pain made me shake harder. "I hope Rex is okay."

Gage leaned down and kissed the top of my head. "Rex will be fine. Let's worry about you right now."

"Okay." I swallowed hard, every inch of me trembling and suddenly so cold. "I can't stop shaking."

"It's shock, princess. Just hang on. I'll take care of you."

Which sounded really good right then, because I was pretty far past the point of taking care of myself, it seemed.

Chapter Seven

GAGE

My axe wasn't sharp enough, the wood I chopped not hard enough, and the pain in my shoulder from swinging over and over again not strong enough to get my mind off of the shitstorm I'd somehow found myself in.

Sitting in the hospital waiting for the doctors to finish working on Katie's hands had been the longest hours of my life. Not even when I'd been shot, dealing with field medics digging in my shoulder and knowing Bishop was in the same situation, had been as bad. I'd spent every moment by her side, earning enough glares and seething glances from the nurses to fire up my temper. I may have been an asshole to them because of it—okay, I'd *definitely* been an asshole. Didn't matter. No way had I been willing to leave her alone for a second.

I'd been the same when I'd finally gotten her home. Well, not my home. I'd have taken her to my cabin, but it wasn't finished yet. She deserved better than to be cooped up in a construction zone. Her apartment didn't have cameras or security in place, so that hadn't been an option either. I'd taken her to Bishop's, where I could set the alarm system and activate the motion detectors whenever I damn well felt like it. Where I could keep her safe.

For now.

I grabbed another heavy log and set it on the cutting stump, squeezing my hands on the handle of my axe before raising it. Looking for some sort of peace in my head, some sort of pain to push me to the point of clarity. I had a feeling that wouldn't be happening anytime soon, no matter how much wood I cut and stacked for the fireplace.

I'd woken up early, before the sun had crested over the treetops to the east, with my arm half numb and my mood already pretty fucking sour. Crashing on the couch probably hadn't been the best idea, but when I'd carried a sleeping Katie in from the truck the night before, I'd been forced to make an impossible choice. Even as keyed up as I'd been, I'd realized the sleeping arrangements wouldn't be to my liking. I couldn't have put her in Bishop's bed—the idea of her in another man's bed, even my best friend's, hadn't sat right with me. I also couldn't have curled up next to her in mine no matter how much I wanted to. Not without knowing she'd wanted me there. She'd had enough taken from her that night—I wouldn't take her consent away from her.

So I'd tucked her into my bed, and I'd slept on the couch. My shoulder wouldn't be thanking me anytime soon for that decision. Neither would my dick. Both things I could deal with better than the thought of seeing pain in those hazel eyes of hers again.

I was still outside chopping wood—house alarm set and a note saying where I was and how to deal with the alarm system sitting on the pillow next to Katie's in case she woke up—when Deacon's truck pulled into the driveway. My dog was home. A good thing, too. The house had seemed oddly quiet without him following me around.

I rested the axe on my shoulder as Deacon stepped out of the vehicle, Rex jumping down and racing past him to get to me. He knocked into my legs, immediately sliding into a sit position and looking up at me with eyes so dark and excited, I couldn't help but smile.

I crouched down and scratched his ears. Rex practically danced into my arms, whining and licking and basically being a happy dog. I loved that mangy mutt.

"How's my good boy?"

"I'm just fine, thanks for asking," Deacon said, shooting me a smirk as he strolled my way. "How's Katie doing?"

"Second-degree burns on her hand with two spots of concern for third degree. I have to take her back in a couple of days, but she was prescribed enough creams and painkillers to last a year."

"Good. That's a brave girl you've got there."

No shit. Before I could answer him though, something on Rex's white paw caught my attention. I grabbed his leg, settling a hand on his back to hold him in place as I took a good look.

"Something wrong?" Deacon asked.

Yeah, there was. "Looks like blood. He's not cut, though."

"Must have been from the restaurant."

"You get cleanup done?" I asked, rising to my feet.

Deacon nodded. "We made it look like a pressure cooker exploded—that'll cover what happened to Katie and the damage to the doors. The gumbo was a lost cause. The other issues we needed to take care of?" He whistled and held up his hand, wiggling his fingers in the air with a silly expression on his face. "They vanished into thin air."

Which probably meant they were buried someplace no one would think to look for them. Good. "So long as it's done, I don't care where they went."

"I took care of you. No worries." He looked off into the distance, no longer smiling. "So...Camden."

Yeah. "He needs time."

"He needs a kick in the ass and some AA meetings, but that's just my opinion."

He wasn't really wrong. "Hopefully, he can figure his shit out and come home. He belongs here."

"Yeah. He does." He frowned my way, looking me up and down. "You're a terrifying sight standing there with an axe. You got more cleanup to be done or something?"

I waved toward the pile of firewood I'd stacked. "I thought Katie might like a fire to keep her warm."

"Good call," he said, completely deadpan. "Give the burn victim a fire to look at."

I shot the guy a glare but set the axe down anyway. "Okay, smartass."

He just grinned. "Don't blame me because I think these things through. But seriously—I'm heading to Alder's to go over a few things about how to handle this coming week. With Camden gone and, I assume, you on Katie's personal guard duty—"

"Yup." No assuming necessary.

"That's what I figured. Anyway, being down two men means our ranks are too tight to keep up the standard protocols. Finn's going to have to guard solo."

The youngest Kennard brother—also a former addict. Not a good mix when dealing with a motorcycle club that cooked meth. One he'd apparently bought from back when he'd used. "Katie's not working for a few days, so the restaurant will be closed."

"She okay with that?"

Probably not. Still, I shrugged. "Doctor's orders. She needs to rest her hands."

"That'll help, then. Keeps her out of the spotlight and knocks down the number of hours we need to monitor the Main Street part of town."

"You moving Mercy Bell out?" The daughter of the family that owned the hardware store in town. She lived in an apartment over her store with her son—the only people who actually lived on Main Street other than Katie, who rented the second apartment over the store from the Bell family. And Katie wouldn't be going back anytime soon.

"That's one of the things we're talking about tonight," Deacon said. "Alder might see if Mercy and her son can move out to one of his family's properties. It'll alleviate a lot of the need for guards in that area."

It would, and keeping Katie with me—away from the restaurant and her apartment, places her uncle and, therefore, the Soul Suckers knew about—worked in my favor as well. Fuck, I hadn't even mentioned her uncle to Alder.

I needed to amend that mistake. "That reminds me. The guys last night?"

Deacon's eyes snapped to mine. "Yeah?"

"They mentioned Baker. As in, Baker sent them, told them Katie'd be at the restaurant late. They even knew it had something to do with soup."

"Because it was gumbo night."

Everyone in town knew that. "Yeah."

"So either our good sheriff's been spying or—"

"Or someone's got some seriously loose lips."

"You think she told him anything? He is her uncle, after all."

And wasn't that the question. "I don't know. Not

intentionally—I can't see her setting up here and starting a business, only to be some sort of traitor to the town."

Deacon nodded, looking just as doubtful about that possibility as I was. "But maybe in passing."

"Right. Good ol' Uncle calls her up, and she fills him in on her life here."

"You ask her about him yet?"

"Nope."

"You going to?"

I wished I could have answered in the negative. "Yeah. Eventually."

"Well, don't wait too long, man. Women get real cranky when they think you're hiding something from them."

Except I wasn't hiding shit—I was giving her time to heal. Totally different things. "You an expert on women now?"

"Expert no, but I do have a second date with Miss Felicia tomorrow."

The liquor store clerk from Rock Falls and my personal weather girl as she had a degree in meteorology and an obsession with researching the models for the local weather patterns. She was also quite a bit younger than the man before me. "You finally gotten over the age difference thing, old man?"

"Not in the least. She talks about when she had a crush on someone named Bieber. What sort of name is that?"

"No clue. But hey, good luck figuring it out."

"Yeah, this old man will need it." Deacon shook his head, looking almost pissed at the thought of having to google this guy. But really, he wasn't that much older than Felicia. He also didn't need any luck, but he wouldn't be hearing that from me.

"Tell Alder about Baker, okay? Tell him to text me if he thinks of anything or needs to know more. No calls, though. I don't want the phone to wake up Katie, and I really don't want her to overhear me talking about her uncle."

"Understood." Deacon held out his fist, bumping my knuckles when I matched his move. "You did good last night, man."

Not even close. "I killed two men in front of a civilian, and I got her burned."

"You got her *out*. Big picture."

Yeah, right. Big picture view, I kept her from being kidnapped and likely killed. I still got her burned and made her watch me kill two men. Not things that would usually endear me to a woman who knew nothing about warfare and combat.

But still, as Deacon hopped into his truck and drove off, heading for Alder's place down the road, I couldn't help but feel a little better. Deacon was right about one thing—I'd gotten Katie out. I'd fought those fuckers and gotten her to safety.

Now I just had to keep doing it.

"Gage?"

I spun at Katie's voice, my heart dive-bombing my stomach. She stood in the doorway to Bishop's house, looking so damn beautiful in the morning light with a blanket wrapped around her shoulders. Even my dog abandoned me to head for her, racing across the yard and jumping onto the wood porch without a backward glance. I'd always known he was the smartest dog on earth.

And I was an idiot for leaving her alone even for a second. "Everything okay?"

"Yeah, I just woke up and..."

And she was alone in a strange house. "Sorry—the temperature's supposed to drop tonight, and I thought you might like a fire."

She pulled her blanket a little tighter around her shoulders, her face suspiciously blank. "Oh. So...I'm staying here again?"

"Yeah. Is that okay?"

Another shrug. Another blank look my way. I abandoned my wood chopping and took off my gloves, heading to the porch slowly. Giving her time to talk if she needed to. Letting her have her space. At least, until I stood right before her.

I simply had to touch her, so I wrapped my fingers around the back of her neck, my thumb running along her jaw. "What's wrong, princess?"

She crinkled her nose but leaned into my touch, something I found fascinating. "Nothing. I think it was just...I woke up, and the house was so silent. I didn't know what was happening or what to do." She licked her lips, her voice fading as she whispered, "I didn't know where you were."

And that probably scared her. "I won't leave you alone again."

"Promise?"

Fuck, those big, doe eyes killed me. "Promise. Now, come on. How about we head inside and watch some sort of cooking channel all afternoon? I might even make you popcorn."

Her grin restored the places inside of me that the pain on her face last night had broken. Put everything back together. "Sounds perfect."

It wasn't—nothing would be perfect until I got rid of the threat against her—but it was something. Spending a lazy day on the couch, I could do. Small and simple, but something she needed and would appreciate.

One step on the path to making her understand just how much I'd do for her.

Chapter Eight

KATIE

Three days. The burns on my hand hurt for a solid seventy-two hours. Pounding the first, aching until I actually cried the second, and moving into highly uncomfortable on the third. By the fourth day, the skin still felt tight, but the pain had dulled to a low roar and I felt back to my old self.

Almost. Because Gage Shepherd had taken my world and flipped it upside down. He'd moved me in to Bishop Kennard's house, claiming it was more secure than my own place. I'd been fine with that—my apartment over the hardware store, while nice enough, had never felt like a home. Maybe it was too beige, or maybe I just wasn't there enough, spending all my time at the restaurant instead. Whatever, leaving that place behind didn't bother me. What did was the fact that I seemed to be taking up all of Gage's time. He woke me every morning with my pain pills and the burn creams I had to apply to my hand, stayed with me all day, and even made sure I was comfortable before I went to sleep. He rarely left my side.

He hadn't kissed me again, though. Hadn't wanted to share his bed with me either. Even when I'd hinted that I was afraid, he'd simply told me he was there—that he was guarding me—and I had nothing to worry about. That quick dismissal stung... sometimes more than my hands did.

"Don't you have to go to work?" I asked on day four as I waited for him to open the back door at the restaurant. My nerves felt frayed and my temper short. Alder had come to tell me about the damage at my place, but I needed to see it for myself. To know if it was truly something I could fix or...not. I hated the idea of *not*.

"I *am* at work. Hang on to my belt, okay?" Gage inched ahead, a gun at the ready. Not *his* gun, at least not the one he'd had the last time we'd been in the restaurant. Rock had taken that one before running off. No, this had to be a different gun, though I couldn't have said what made it different.

So, yeah...Gage had a gun in his hand and his dog on his heels as he made sure it was safe for us to go inside. I did as I was told, holding on to him as I followed him and Rex through the back hallway. The doors into the kitchen had been broken almost off the hinges, no longer looking as if a shotgun blast had torn through them. Something bigger and stronger had to have done that sort of damage—the explosion of a pressure cooker, apparently. I wasn't ready to think about that just yet.

"Sitting in the restaurant with me all day is your job now? You get paid for this?" My stomach dropped when Gage's step stuttered almost imperceptibly. Something that seemed ridiculous—his earning a salary while guarding me—was actually quite likely because this was Justice. The Kennard family took care of their people, and Gage was definitely one of their people.

"Oh my god, you *get paid* for this. To sit around, do nothing, and watch over me. Even when we're at Bishop's place and you're watching SportsCenter? That seems excessive, don't you think? Alder has to be losing so much money, and it's all my fault. Well, not really my fault, only kind of my fault. I didn't come here with guns blazing ready to steal someone away—they did. Those Soul Suckers. Still, I feel so bad. What if they need you at the mill? What if a machine goes down and someone gets hurt? What if—"

"Katie."

Seriously, interrupting me to shut me up was both the best and worst thing the man could do. I hadn't babbled like that in days—not once while we'd been holed up at Bishop's place. But this was different—this was looking over the remains of the business I'd built, the one I'd left Denver to start when I'd realized how much I'd missed the safety of a town like Justice. The one that had brought me so much joy even as the long hours and constant workload had left me drifting without anyone to hang on to for security.

Except Gage, who stared at me as I wrangled my nerves into submission and took a deep breath. "Sorry."

He didn't look away, didn't shy away from the issue at all. "I don't get paid to watch you. Not really. And it wouldn't matter if Alder kept my checks coming or not—your safety is my first priority."

How the man could make me melt when everything inside of me felt so frazzled, I had no idea. But he did. Especially when he took a step closer, grabbing my neck in that way he did, the roughness of his hand scraping against my jaw as he held me in place. Looked down at me with an intensity in his eyes that pushed everything else away.

"I won't let anything happen to you," he said, his voice like gravel—rough and gritty. Weathered but strong. And I believed him.

"Okay."

"Good. Now hang here for a second, and I'll make sure the kitchen is clear." Gage didn't move though, not at first. He kept staring at me instead, kept his face right in front of mine. Kept me on the balls of my feet as I waited for *something*—waited for the kiss I could practically feel coming. The one I'd been craving for four very long days.

The one he still wouldn't give me.

Frowning, he eventually let me go, pulled back with stiff, short steps as if every one of them hurt. They hurt me too. I was too afraid to say that, though. A deep breath, then Gage gave a hand signal to Rex so the dog would stay right next to my legs, and he disappeared through the destroyed doors. My heart rate spiked, my body tingling as I waited for him to return. As I fought the rising panic inside of me at being away from him.

It didn't take him long even if it felt like a lifetime. Within what had to be only seconds, he was back and grabbing my arm. Keeping his eyes locked on mine as my hands shook and my nerves jumped into high gear. As he pulled me through the doors and gave me space to walk into...

My kitchen.

The prep table looked completely warped, sitting against the wall at a rakish angle as if something had moved it quite suddenly. The pass-through shelves had a definite wave to them, but nothing a rubber mallet and some elbow grease wouldn't fix. The stove and flat top appeared completely normal, and the fryer even seemed ready to go. I'd expected way worse.

I let out the breath I'd been holding in a loud whoosh. "It doesn't look as bad as I thought it would."

"Deacon figured the pressure cooker could have been one of

those electric ones." He pointed, directing me to see the popular electric countertop appliance wedged into the wall across the room. "That kept the explosion at this end of the space and left your machines in working order."

"I thought everything would be destroyed."

"We wouldn't have done that to you, princess. Not unless there'd been no other way."

I couldn't help it. I ran at him, jumping and clinging to his neck as he grabbed my hips and held me tight. I hadn't even realized how anxious I'd been. Hadn't acknowledged the fear within me. When Alder had told me they'd faked an explosion, I'd assumed they had ruined everything and I'd have to start all over again. Buy new equipment and tools, close the restaurant for months as I tried to find the money to rebuild.

This was nothing like I'd expected.

"Thank you," I whispered, my forehead pressing against his chest. "Thank you for not destroying my business."

Gage chuckled. "You can thank Alder and Deacon—they spent a lot of time figuring out how they could make the story look real while saving your equipment." He held me a little tighter, his hands hot where they'd slid up under my shirt. "Maybe just don't thank them like this, okay?"

"Never."

"Good." He patted my ass, unwrapping himself from around me and setting me back on my feet. "Now, wait here. I want to check out the dining room."

He set Rex to guard me again, then disappeared through the mostly undamaged doors to the dining room. A good coat of paint and those would be back to looking perfect. Easy enough. Not an ideal situation—I hated that my place was closed and would need to be for at least a few more days—but not as bad as I'd thought. The men had truly taken care of me.

God, I loved living in Justice.

Gage stormed back into the kitchen, gun still drawn and a fierce look on his face. His "clearing the room" expression. With his wild beard and overall scary demeanor, most people wouldn't have noticed the way his eyes softened when he saw me. How the shadow of fear disappeared when he verified I was still safely tucked away with his dog. Most people in town wouldn't see how much the man worried.

I saw. I saw too much.

"What's the plan?" he asked as he holstered his gun once more.

I shrugged. "Clean up, I guess. I figure I can put the prep table back to rights and make sure all my gear is cleaned before I do anything too strenuous."

"You need me?" he asked, and though I knew he meant to help, my mind spun in a different direction. Yes, I needed him. To hold me again, kiss me the way he had that night in the gym, make me feel something other than fear and panic and the residual crappiness of not knowing when the Soul Suckers would strike again.

I couldn't say all that, though. "Just to pull the table over. I can handle the rest. You can be off duty this morning."

His lips quirked into a smile as he headed across the room to drag the heavy stainless-steel table back to where it belonged. He barely strained, his muscles bulging but his face calm as he pulled. So strong, this man. So filled with testosterone. I loved it.

Once the prep table sat back in place, Gage settled onto his stool. After a single hand signal to Rex, the dog raced across the room and leaned against his calves. Both watching me. Two sets of dark eyes following my every move. I'd have said the attention made me uncomfortable, but that would be a lie. Maybe before the night of the attack, it would have, but no longer. Now? I felt guarded. Almost safe. Almost.

It didn't take me long to find my groove. I loaded everything I could into the industrial dishwasher, leaving the things I couldn't sitting on the counter. Someone would have to wash those—not me. Gage had made sure to tell me I wasn't allowed to put my hands in hot, soapy water. Which worked fine for me. Even the idea of that made my burns hurt.

I was halfway through the wash cycle, restocking pans along the shelves at the bottom of the table, when the back doorbell rang. The pan I'd been holding dropped to the floor, clattering across the tiles. My breath caught, and I spun around, reaching for the table edge to hold myself up. Seeking out the mountain man in the corner on an almost instinctual level. Gage was up and across the kitchen like a shot, his gun back in his hand. His eyes locked on what was left of the heavy swinging doors. Protecting me. Guarding me.

Calming me.

When the initial panic began to subside, the pieces of days and times and schedules fell into place. I was an idiot. A forgetful idiot. "It's my produce delivery. I didn't have time to cancel it."

Gage glanced at me before looking into the back hallway again. A quick, "Rex, guard," and he disappeared through the doors, heading toward the alley entrance where—hopefully—my produce delivery driver didn't look too threatening.

I did my best to control my breathing, to keep the panic at bay. Rex helped, but this was just another pattern I'd learned over the last few days. If Gage was out of my sight, I worried. Once he came back into the room, the majority of that would go away. Not all...just most. The only time I truly felt safe was when I sat close enough to Gage to feel his heat, to touch. We weren't doing any of that intentionally, but sometimes his arm brushed mine as we watched TV on the couch, or he sat on the edge of the bed to help me apply the burn cream and his leg would rest against mine. Those times...yeah, I lived for them.

Gage appeared at the kitchen doors, his eyes on me as he let a man through with a hand truck stacked with boxes. My normal delivery driver—the same guy from the only restaurant supply company in the county whom I'd met while setting up the restaurant months ago. The order looking about the same size as I always got. Nothing out of the ordinary. Everything back to the new normal.

Except I could barely breathe, and my hands wouldn't stop shaking. I did my best to hide that, though. "Hey, Charlie."

Charlie grinned and shot me a wink. Old normal. Before the attack, I would have laughed and flirted, knowing the guy was happily married and it meant nothing. Now? New normal? I had a hard time pulling a smile for him.

He didn't seem to notice, though. "Miss Katie. You're looking lovely this morning. What happened to your hands?"

Because I had white bandages under gloves on each to keep them clean. I shot a glance at Gage, but he was busy staring down Charlie. Figured. "I, uh, had an accident in the kitchen. You know there's no way to avoid getting burned."

"I do. I know that well." Charlie looked over my shoulder—at Gage, I assumed—and his smile fell.

"You doing okay?" he asked, suddenly looking concerned. "I noticed you weren't open, and those doors look—"

"They look like none of your goddamned business," Gage said, a deep growl to his voice. He stood behind Charlie, arms crossed over his broad chest, a scowl on his face. Scary soldier mode in effect.

"It's okay," I said, though whether to Charlie or Gage, I

couldn't say. "I was a little careless, and a pressure cooker exploded. One of those electric ones, you know?"

Charlie nodded. "My wife has one. I thought they were supposed to be safer than the stovetop ones."

I held up my hands and shrugged. "So did I. But at least it just ruined the back doors and not my stove, right?"

"Yeah. Right." He didn't seem convinced, but he also didn't matter. Gage did, and he looked positively lethal. Even Rex appeared ready to attack—his ears up, back straight, and standing still as a statue beside his owner. Ready to fight, the both of them.

"You know," Charlie said, still looking awfully uncomfortable under Gage's scrutiny. "If I call the boss, I might be able to take some of this stuff back."

I was removing my plastic gloves and shaking my head before he finished. That would take more time, and I just wanted him gone. "No need. If I don't open today or tomorrow, I'll hold a giveaway for my customers. That food won't go to waste."

Charlie nodded, pulling out the tablet he used to verify orders. Faster than any other time before, Charlie ran through my list, pointing to each box in turn as he pulled off the lids to show me the contents before setting them next to the walk-in. We kept a casual sort of conversation going—how nicely the kale was coming in for the region, the upcoming winter weather forecasts, the flooding that had hit the area at the end of the rainy season. Nothing deep or personal, yet something about the way Gage watched us—the way he watched *me*—caused my heart to race and my cheeks to stay flushed. Charlie seemed to feel it as well—the man hauled ass out the door the second I'd signed for my delivery.

I'd never been so happy to see Charlie leave...at least until Gage spoke again.

"You were nervous around him."

"What?"

Gage moved closer, all long legs and smooth strides, ending in a lean against the other side of the counter. Bracing his arms on the stainless-steel top and causing the muscles in his biceps and forearms to flex. "Charlie made you nervous."

I had to tear my eyes away from his arms. From the patterns of color and shading creating pictures all along his skin. "He never did before, but today..."

"Today was different."

I nodded.

"But even before today, I made you nervous."

Oh. That observation brushed against something I didn't want to talk about, the attraction to him I'd tried to deny. But four days of him sleeping on the couch and taking care of me had busted a hole through my filter, so I answered honestly. Unable not no. "You do sometimes, yeah."

The way he cocked his head sent a shiver of anticipation up my spine. "Why?"

"You're a bit intimidating."

He frowned. "Intimidating."

"Yes. Intimidating. Your size and the beard and the whole wild thing you've got going on." I waved my hand in a circle to encompass the *him* I meant. "Intimidating."

With the look of a predator hunting his prey, he stalked around the counter. Staring hard. His eyes pinning me in place. He didn't stop until he had me trapped against the counter, until he brushed my body with his. Until he was close enough for me to feel the heat from him through my clothes.

Safe. I felt safe, even if he was the most dangerous man I'd ever met.

"I never wanted to intimidate you."

I couldn't think, couldn't breathe. So close, so very, very

close. Like the other night in the gym—when he'd kissed me. When he'd pushed me right to the brink with his hands and his mouth and those dirty words he'd said. I would have done anything to relive that moment with a better ending, would have given up almost anything for another chance at getting him alone and in that position. But if I understood the heat burning deep in his gaze, I might not have to give up anything.

I licked my bottom lip, watching as his eyes tracked the movement. "You may not mean to intimidate me, but you do. It's simply part of you being you."

He hummed and leaned over me, making my heart race. Making my breath catch as my nipples tightened and my skin itched for his touch. Every sense heightened, every feeling multiplied, until I was a shaking mess of girl right on the edge of... something. Something I'd been craving for days.

Gage stopped as his lips came close enough to brush mine, as his breath whispered across them with every word. "Is this intimidating?"

"No."

"You're shaking."

I was. "Because I want you so much."

His lips kicked up into a cocky sort of smile, one that encapsulated the man before me. But that expression faded fast, and in the next second, he kissed me. Pressed himself against me from head to toe, wrapped his arms around my body, and positively took control of my mouth. Soft and sweet, the kiss lingered, growing in intensity then fading. His hands clutching my hips then softening to stroke me gently. Too gently.

"I won't break," I murmured when he retreated again. When he groaned and moved as if to end the kiss. Not happening. I tugged him closer, trying to rise onto the balls of my feet to reach him. Trying to beg for more with my actions instead of my words.

But Gage was nothing if not in control. He refused to give in, holding me at bay even as he brushed his lips against mine one more time. As he gripped my flesh in a bruising hold.

"I don't want to hurt you."

Him pulling away hurt. It hurt so bad. "You made me a promise. Told me what you were going to do to me the next time you got me alone."

Gage froze, staring down at me with a fire burning behind his eyes. "I promised to lick you all over."

"You're late on delivery."

With a growl, he grabbed me by the back of the thighs and lifted me, setting my ass on the edge of the counter before licking a path down my neck. He took from me, his grip tight and his kisses harder. Wilder than before. And fuck, did I love it.

He spread me wide, forcing his body between my legs. Making room. But oh my god, his mouth. So hot. So good. So fucking filthy.

"Is that a reminder to lick your pretty pussy, princess? I'm pretty sure that's what I said I'd do—lick you until you were good and wet, then suck your little clit. Own it. I said I'd beg for it, didn't I? I will, too. Because trust me, it's all I've been thinking about."

Oh god, his hands felt so good on my body, his beard rough against my skin in a way that I'd somehow missed. "Then why haven't you even kissed me?"

"You've been recovering."

"I only burned my hands, not the rest of me."

He laughed, the rumble more something I felt than heard. "You're right. I've been remiss in my attention." He slid a hand up my leg, all the way up. Not stopping until his fingers pressed against my pussy. Traced it. Circled my clit and made me moan and arch and wish for more. I might have been the one begging at that point.

But Gage was the one promising to take care of me. "I've wanted to lick you so bad these last few days, but I thought you were hurting too much so I left you alone." He pressed his thumb against my clit, the pressure hard and rough just like him. And so, so good. "I'm going to fix that right now."

Chapter Nine

GAGE

I was a fucking animal.

I didn't even get Katie naked, didn't even strip her pants off so I could lavish her pussy with attention. I just yanked the tight, stretchy, teasing piece of fabric she wore down her legs and pushed her knees up and apart as far as I could, giving me enough room to finally see what I'd been dreaming about for weeks. To look over what I was about to claim.

Pink. So much pink. A small strip of dark curls—close-cropped and neat—practically pointed to the promised land, but the rest? Bare. Slick and swollen and so damn soft-looking.

Fucking mine.

"Your cunt is so pretty, princess." I dropped down to tease her, running my nose along the flesh of her belly on my way to her pussy. Letting the scrape of my beard raise goose bumps like I knew it would. "Just as pink and wet as I've been dreaming about."

"Gage, please." Katie grabbed my hair and tugged, trying to direct me where she wanted me. Trying to drive this train. Not yet, though. Not quite yet. I needed to take a breath and enjoy the moment for what it was. A start to something. An ending to the past and a new beginning. Fuck yeah, I was all in on that.

Katie moaned and tugged and arched into me, though. Trying her hardest but holding back her words. That wouldn't do. The girl babbled when she was nervous—she'd probably said a million words to me, most of them nonsense. I wanted her to say what she meant, what she felt and thought and needed. I wanted her words so badly; the need had created a pit of yearning in my soul too deep to see the bottom of.

As I stroked her inner thigh and brushed my beard across her pale skin, I wondered if that was how she felt around me. All pent up and craving some fucking words, some syllables and sounds. I held my tongue around her because I knew if I spoke, the filthiest shit in my imagination would come out. Things like how I liked that she was small enough for me to hold up and fuck against the wall. How I wondered if her pussy would let my cock in easy or if I'd have to take it slow at first, if I could pound her right away or if I needed to go gentle until I had her good and warmed up. If I let go, I would have told her how I dreamed of licking up every drop of her pussy, that thoughts of what she tasted like when she was close to coming tended to overtake my mind and force me to jack off two and three times a day.

I didn't need to say that last one anymore because I was about to find out. The rest? Well, maybe it was time to let her hear a little from me.

"Fucking dreamed of this," I said, unable to hold back for another second. "Stripping you bare and spreading you out like a feast for a king. Your king—the only man who gets to partake of this bounty. And it is a bounty, sweet princess. All that pink skin, so soft and swollen and wet for me. Fuck baby, I'm going to come just from looking at that beautiful cunt. I've been dying to taste this pussy. I'm going to lick every fucking inch of you."

So I did, and the taste of her, the heat on my tongue and the way she responded to my touch, was as perfect as I'd known it would be. I licked her from opening to clit, teasing the little bud before dropping back to where I started. Refusing to ease off but not ready to go flat out on her clit and make her come just yet. Not ready to give her what she needed to get off. She wanted to, though. That was for sure. She bucked and tugged my hair, whispering my name and all those beautiful words I'd long wanted her to say like please and more and good and fuck. My beautiful, filthy girl.

As she grew louder and the curse words flew more freely, I held her down and doubled my efforts. Kept my hand on her hips and her thighs spread around me. Kept my mouth sucking on her pussy and my tongue lashing at her clit as I passed it. Weeks...I'd been obsessed with being exactly where I found myself for weeks. No fucking way was I taking a shortcut now. No way was I missing a single fucking second of tasting her.

I wasn't rushing this either. Instead, I took my goddamned time, lavishing her with slow licks and sucks. With brushes of my beard against her flesh and plunging my fingers deep inside her to tease even that hidden little bundle of nerves I knew would have her screaming in no time. I lapped every drop of wetness she gave me, licking up all her juices and causing more as I teased and fucked and suckled. And in between those moves, when I knew she needed an extra little push toward her impending orgasm, I'd head up to tease her clit. To suck hard on the little bud and attack it with my tongue. She liked that for sure. She'd moan and cry out, grab my hair tighter, and rock her hips against me. Riding my fucking mouth as if this was the best pussy-eating she'd ever had. Good, because now that I'd claimed her cunt? Now that I'd seen it, felt it, tasted every inch? I'd be the last bastard to ever give her this. The only one to know just how sweet what she hid between her thighs truly was.

I was a lucky fucking man.

"I can't wait for you to ride my face," I said before flattening my tongue against her clit for a good, deep lick. "I want to see your hips rocking, taking what you need from me. Want to drown in your wetness, princess. Do you have any idea how soaked you are right now? All from me. It's dripping down onto this table thing. Such a waste. I'd rather drink it all down. Let you sit right over my mouth so I don't miss a drop."

I sucked hard on her clit, twisting my fingers inside her and thrusting deep. My hips rocked, my body unable to stop. I couldn't wait to get inside her, to plunge my cock deep into her cunt and feel her tighten all around me. The need to bury myself in her warmth so strong. The want to fuck her pussy almost too much to resist. Almost. Because there was no way I wasn't making my girl come on my mouth first.

Katie groaned something that sounded like my name, writhing under my touch. Tugging hard on my hair as she rocked her hips against me. As she fucked my face hard.

I groaned and slid another finger inside her, working that third digit in to give her a little more pressure. "Fuck, princess. You're so tight and soft. Your sweet little cunt is going to crush my cock, isn't it? It's going to take me hours to break in this pussy enough to take all of me, isn't it?"

Katie's eyes met mine, so bright and hot—hooded with lust and need and desire. I couldn't look away. I slid my fingers out and back in, pressed my thumb against her clit to give her what she needed to get off. And when I had her staring, when her body trembled and arched into my touch, when she was riding my hand without hesitation or embarrassment, I took my thumb away, leaned down, and sucked her clit into my mouth.

She came with a yelp that turned into an almost wordless sort of chant. Almost, because my name was definitely in there a handful of times, making me feel like a king as I pushed her through every second of her orgasm. I kept teasing her, kept dragging her through it as her cunt pulsed around my fingers, as I dreamed of that feeling around my cock. As I fought off my own need to come so I could make sure she got hers first.

Besides, my cock needed to stand the fuck down. I wouldn't be fucking her in this kitchen. Not for our first time. I wanted her relaxed and warm, naked and comfortable. I wanted her in my bed, to be honest. My bed...at my cabin. Not the one I borrowed at Bishop's place. Not his couch where I wouldn't be sleeping again if I had my way. And definitely not on some stainless-steel counter in the kitchen of her restaurant where she'd just watched me kill two fuckers a few days before. That wasn't going to happen, so I'd have to control myself.

My dick was none too pleased with that decision.

"I can't," Katie said, her voice all breathy and soft as she pushed me off her. As her clenching turned to quivers and her muscles finally quieted enough not to try to strangle me. I pulled my hand from her but wasn't ready to let her go completely, so I snuggled against her lower belly and kept my hands on her thighs. I even kissed her hip bone.

The little shiver she gave at that almost made me laugh. "You okay?"

I felt the vibration of her chuckle more than heard it. "Yeah. Okay works for how I feel right now."

Good. I'd take that. I tickled my fingers up and down her thighs, taking a moment to just be. To allow myself to feel her against me and enjoy the taste of her lingering on my lips. To feel her heat and know that I did that—I had gotten her hot and bothered, had worked her pussy well and made her come all over me. Had owned that fucking cunt as a good man should.

My pussy.

My princess.

My heart.

Katie groaned after a while, though, pulling herself to sitting and forcing me to give up my spot. "I think you killed me."

I placed one last kiss on her thigh before helping her to sit up. "I'd prefer to keep you alive."

"Yeah, well..." The mood shifted, her brow furrowing and her smile dropping. She hopped down off the counter, tugging her pants into place as soon as her feet hit the floor. Covering up. I hated that, but her mind was already elsewhere.

"You think they'll come back for me, don't you?"

They. The Soul Suckers. I grabbed her wrist, needing to touch, being careful with her damaged hand, though. "I think they're sick bastards."

"That didn't answer my question."

No, it didn't. "I won't let them near you."

She gave me a frustrated sort of scowl, but I wasn't having it. I grabbed her other wrist and tugged both, wanting her closer. Needing to feel her again. Always. I pulled her arms around me and settled them so she held me close. And when I had her pressed against me, when she practically melted into me, I leaned down to get a taste of her lips. Just one. A sweet one. I'd eaten her out like an animal, but I could be gentler with her. I should be.

Katie smiled when we broke apart, bringing her hand to the side of my face. Scratching her fingers into my beard. "You need a trim."

I...wasn't expecting that. "I do?"

Her eyes went wide, and I knew she'd be babbling before she even opened her mouth.

"It's not that I don't like the mountain man thing you've got going on"—her face flushed when I raised my eyebrows at that one—"it's just that you're so wild looking. Sometimes, I can't see your expression, so I don't know what to think about...well, anything really. But that wouldn't bother me except you look so big and hard." Silence. For one beat, nothing but silence as her face went red and she seemed to realize just what she'd said. "Oh my god, not big...there. And hard not like hard...you probably are, though, aren't you? And I didn't do anything to fix that or to help you out because I was too lost in my own thing. I'm so sorry, I'm the worst fuck buddy in the history of the world because—"

I pressed my lips to hers, fighting hard not to laugh. The girl was adorable when she felt flustered. And this time, I wasn't gentle. I kissed her deep, slicking my tongue against hers to get a taste. Holding her body against mine and letting her feel just how big and hard I was. For her. Always for her.

When I finally backed away, released her mouth from my attack, I kissed the tip of her nose and murmured, "I'll get it trimmed."

"You don't have to."

"I know. I want to."

The smile she gave me was everything. "Okay."

Okay. That was enough to make me feel like I'd done something right for her, like I was a king making sure my queen had everything she needed. Like I was a *man* and had pleased my woman. Fuck, this curvy little girl wrecked me, and I loved every second of it.

What I didn't love was hearing the bell over the front door peal.

Katie stiffened when she heard it, reaching out to grab hold of my sides. "Did you—"

"Nope." I grabbed my gun out of the holster under my arm but almost immediately put it back. Alder was not a stupid man, and he had a voice that carried well.

"Gage. It's Alder and Shye. We're coming back." Alder opened the door from the dining room slowly, making sure he had my attention before swinging it wide and ushering Shye inside the kitchen. "Hey, man. Sorry—I saw your truck out back and figured you two would be in here. I used my key without thinking about it."

He could have gotten himself shot for that one, not that I needed to remind him of that. He wouldn't have apologized if he hadn't already realized his mistake. "What's up?"

By the way he glanced at Katie, I knew I wouldn't like what he had to say.

"I've been texting, but you didn't answer. They need you at the job site."

Definitely didn't like that. "No."

Alder's blue eyes went hard, his irritation at being challenged obvious. "The delimber's down again. The crew can't finish the harvest without it, and no one on your team can figure out what's wrong with the thing. Hunter said something about some parts that came in yesterday, but I didn't want him trying to replace them without your guidance. We've got two more days max of work left to do, and then we can shut the site down. Help us out here."

For about a second, I wasn't sure which to be more pissed about—that I had to leave Katie's side, or that someone had touched that delimber and likely messed it up worse than when they started. And Hunter—I'd kick his ass if he tried to replace those fuel injectors. He could make the entire engine seize if he fucked that up. Katie won out as the thing I was most pissed about, though. And the thing I was most concerned about as well.

"You backing me up?" I ran my hand up Katie's arm, making sure he got my point. That he knew what was at stake.

Alder didn't seem to need the reminder. "I'll handle it."

I shot a look at Katie, unable not to. She was my weakness—I'd admit that any day of the week—but she made me stronger too. More focused. I'd wreck the fucking world to protect her.

Alder Kennard had better be ready to do the same.

"Be sure, boss," I said, holding Alder's gaze. Setting my challenge, my rules, at his feet. He couldn't waffle on this—if I was going to leave, he needed to be prepared to lay down his life for not just his girl but mine. Hard thing for an average man to agree to.

Alder wasn't average. "I've got your back. No matter what."

That was the best I'd get.

Turning my back on Alder and Shye, I grabbed Katie and pulled her close. Needing to get my fill before I had to leave her. "I have to go to work."

"Okay."

Her voice sounded anything but okay, and the tremble in her hands didn't argue that. She might not have been babbling away, but she was nervous. So was I, to be honest. Leaving her was the last thing I wanted to do.

"Alder will take care of you." Whether I was soothing Katie or myself, I couldn't tell. Didn't seem to work, though. She simply grabbed me tighter, and I curled over her. Covering her with my body as much as possible. Holding her tight.

Fuck, this was a bad idea.

Katie simply repeated herself, though. "Okay."

Still not good.

"You're killing me, princess." I picked her up and carried her into the walk-in refrigerator, closing the door behind us so we had a little privacy. Even if that privacy came with a bit of a chill. I knew how to keep my girl warm. I wrapped myself around her smaller form and pulled her in tight. "Will you be okay without me here? Tell the truth."

"Of course I will." But she wasn't looking at me. That shit had to stop.

I ran a finger up her throat and along her chin, lifting until those hazel eyes met mine. Until they had to. "You can come with me. It's wet and dirty and in the middle of a fucking forest, but you can watch me work if that helps."

She sighed, still not looking completely comfortable. "I have too much to do. Besides, I'll be fine. Alder will be here with me."

My girl had her game face on for sure, but I saw through it. Probably because I felt the same unease she did. Alder wasn't me —he wouldn't take as good care of her as I did. Or at least, that's what my instincts screamed at me. But the sooner I left, the sooner I could get back to her. And then, I wouldn't let her leave my side again.

"Okay," I said, reaching up to brush the side of her breast where I knew her phone was tucked away. Those sinful pants she'd been wearing didn't have pockets. I still loved them, though. Mostly because of the way they hugged her ass. "Text me if you need anything. Anything at all. You hear me?"

She nodded once, but that fear—that gleam in her eyes—was too much. I leaned down and kissed her deep, licking my way into her mouth for one last taste. One solid promise that I'd be back for more.

And then I let her go before I couldn't.

I tugged her behind me as I stalked back through the kitchen, glaring Alder's way with every step. Making sure he knew exactly what was coming if he didn't live up to his promise. The man stood solid and sure, his girl tucked against his side, his eyes not leaving mine. An oath in his stance.

One I was going to be forced to take at face value.

I kissed Katie one more time as I directed her into her little cooking area, and then I said the only words left to say.

"Rex, guard."

Without a backward glance, I walked out of the kitchen and through the back door without my girl or my dog at my side. Just a heavy boulder in my stomach and a clock counting down in my head.

Chapter Ten

GAGE

My irritation at Alder had reached the point of explosion as I stepped out of The Baker's Cottage. I definitely needed to get the fuck out before I went back in there and grabbed Katie, told Alder to fuck off, and got the hell out of town. But when I looked down the alley, instead of a straight shot to my parking spot in the back, I saw Bishop's smug face behind the windshield of his truck.

Irritation turned to curiosity, but that didn't stop me from beelining it in his direction.

"Thought you were coming back tomorrow," I said as I hopped into the passenger seat. "Alder know you're here?"

"You really think my brother would send you to a job site when Katie's at risk?"

No. Probably not, which finally turned my anger into a feeling close to excitement. Mission time. "So, what's the situation?"

"We found Rock."

Motherfucker. The man who'd grabbed Katie, who'd caused her to burn her hands, who'd stolen my gun. The afternoon was looking up. "Where?"

"He's at the Soul Suckers clubhouse over the county line. We've got about forty minutes before he's set to leave. Some sort of errand for the Pres. Parris promises he'll be alone."

Parris. Deacon's friend, former Marine, and a member of a motorcycle club himself, though not the Soul Suckers. I didn't care for any of them, though—didn't matter the colors on their backs. Not after all that had happened in the last few months. But Alder and Deacon trusted Parris, so I'd follow their lead... Until he proved me wrong.

I buckled in as Bishop pulled out of the alley. "Katie's going to know something's up if Anabeth comes strolling into the restaurant."

"She won't be," he said, his words clipped and concise. "Finn's keeping an eye on her at my place."

His youngest brother, former addict, and the man who'd almost killed Anabeth back in high school. True, it'd been somewhat accidental—no way the kid could have known she'd react so badly to whatever drug they'd been doing at the time— but that didn't mean Bishop had forgiven him. Or trusted him.

"You sure that's a good idea?"

"Fuck no, but she's sick, and I wasn't leaving her in Vegas. Deacon's on the roof keeping an eye on Main Street while we take care of this shit, and Camden's MIA, so Finn gets the job."

Ah, so Alder assigned him there. No wonder Bishop was so pissed about it. "So this will be a quick job—in and out."

"Abso-fucking-lutely. No way am I leaving Anabeth alone overnight."

Good, because Katie wasn't spending a whole night without me around either. "So what's Alder's plan?"

"Alder isn't laying out the rules today. It's you and me." Bishop held out his fist, giving me the chance to bump it as he roared down the highway. "We do this our way. Show up, grab the guy, beat the fuck out of him, and get your gun back. Easy."

"Nothing's ever that easy."

"Yeah, well, we've got women to get home to, so we're going to have to make it that easy."

———

The plan went better than I would have expected. Rock left the clubhouse just as Parris had said he would—at the right time and all alone in his car. No bike, which made our job that much easier. We followed a good distance behind him until he reached a secluded part of the highway, then Bishop played bumper cars with him until he finally drove off the road.

Step one: easy.

My first sighting of the burns on his face—the ones Katie had caused when she hit him with that hot pan—made me both oddly proud and irrationally pissed. Bastard deserved a hell of a lot more for grabbing her, but she'd held her own.

Of course, if I'd been a little faster or more observant, we likely wouldn't have been in a situation where she'd needed to defend herself anyway. That guilt was a heavy burden to carry. I'd make it up to her, though. Starting today.

Gloves on and scowl in place, I tightened my grip on my gun and hurried to the car door with Bishop right on my heels. He'd gone in first when we'd taken out the fucker holding Anabeth hostage. This guy had hurt my girl, so it was my turn to lead the mission.

A job I didn't take lightly. "Get the fuck out of the car, or I'll burn you out."

Rock opened the door, holding his hands above his head and looking like a man who knew his number was up. "You don't want to do this, man."

"Do what? We're not doing anything. We're not even here, are we, Bishop?"

"Nah. Not at all. We're just a figment of your imagination working on getting a little payback."

"See?" I said, keeping my gun trained on Rock as I shrugged. "We're not really here. Consider us like the conscience you obviously don't have—you came for my woman, so whatever we do to you? It's justified. I mean, not that we're going to do anything, since we're not here and all."

"Nope," Bishop said, popping that P like a motherfucker. "Not here. So anything we do? Never happened."

Rock looked from Bishop to me and back again. "He didn't tell us anything about the girl, just to grab her and bring her to him."

"He who?" Bishop asked. Not that I needed the confirmation. I knew the words Rock was going to say before he opened his mouth.

"Baker. He ordered the job."

"And you carried it out." I gave him a grin. "Or you tried to, really. Nice burns, by the way. Bet they hurt like a bitch."

He didn't like that. "Fuck you."

"No thanks. My dick gets enough attention." I nodded at Bishop, the signal that it was time to get down to the business of why we were there. "Where's the gun you stole from me?"

Rock's face went blank, a sure sign he was about to lie his fucking head off. "Don't know what you're talking about."

"You think he's telling the truth, Bish?"

"Not even close."

"Yeah, me neither." With every bit of strength I could muster, I kicked Rock in the knee, enjoying the satisfying crunch of his joint as my boot made contact. Growing even happier when he fell to the ground with an anguished sort of scream. One that wasn't anywhere near as painful to listen to as Katie's had been the night she'd burned her hands. I wanted more from him, and I'd get it. Just as soon as we accomplished our goal. "Where's my fucking gun?"

"In the car," Rock said with a gasp as he curled into the fetal position and clutched his knee. Bishop headed to the other side of the vehicle, tugging on his gloves before opening the passenger door and ducking inside to search. Me? I wasn't done with Rock yet.

"Bet you wish you'd grabbed it when we came up behind you, don't you?"

"Won't matter," he said, uncurling from his position and groaning as he tried to straighten his leg. "Whether I take you out today or one of the other guys does it tomorrow—you're done."

I leaned over, shoving my gun right in his face. "I think you're the one who's done, friend. The only question is how quick we'll make it. Why did Baker want the girl?"

"Don't know. He's had a hard-on for her for years but said he couldn't get her in Boulder or some shit."

Denver, but I didn't need to correct him. "He never mentioned his relationship with her?"

"What relationship?" he said, almost laughing. "The guy wanted her—said she owed him something. That was all I needed to know. I don't plan the jobs, I just get the shit done."

"Not this time." I looked up as Bishop came back around the car.

"Looking for this?" He handed me my gun—my favorite

Beretta—then pointed his own at Rock. "I think we're done here. Unless our friend has anything else he wants to say?"

"Yeah." Rock sat up and leaned against the side of the car, looking awfully pale. "You Justice fucks are all dead. Pistol's going to raze the whole fucking town when he finds out. Maybe not your women, though. He might give them a pass." He looked right at Bishop. "I hear he likes to make the redheads bleed."

I saw Bishop's face change, nearly felt the rage come over him. No way was I making him sit back and watch me do what he wanted to. Katie had gotten her own revenge—so long as the guy was in the ground, I'd have mine. "Take it, B."

Bishop fired one shot—a clean hit to the center of the forehead. Job done. Rock slumped to the side, most likely dead. Though if he wasn't, he would be soon enough.

"How are we handling cleanup?" I asked as I holstered my gun and tucked my Beretta into the back of my jeans. After checking it was unloaded, of course. No sense being an idiot and shooting myself in the ass when I had work to do.

"I say we take him out to the gorge and let his car go over the edge. An unfortunate accident for an unfortunate human."

"You don't think the bullet wound will be a little obvious?"

He shrugged, completely casual as he said, "We'll leave the seat belt off and make sure the fucker burns at the bottom."

That meant going to the bottom with him. "That's a long hike down."

"It's gonna feel like a longer one coming back up, so let's get moving. Trunk?"

I nodded. "Trunk."

We hefted Rock into the trunk of his car, working together to keep the bloody parts away from our clothes. Once done, I slammed the lid and held out a fist to Bishop. "I'll lead. You keep my six clear."

"I do *love* riding your ass."

If I didn't love the man like a brother, I'd likely throw *him* into the gorge. But that would take time—one thing we didn't have enough of. I wanted to get back to Justice, to Katie, and I knew Bishop felt the same about Anabeth. Which was why it took me completely off guard when he pulled me to a stop before I could get behind the wheel of Rock's car.

"You know I've always got your back."

As if I'd ever question that. "Yeah, man. I know."

"No, I mean..." He glanced at the car then back at me. "If shit goes sideways here, I'll be pulling off to get out of the way."

Meaning if it looked like I'd get popped with a dead body in the trunk, he wouldn't be sticking around to help me. It wasn't personal—it was preservation. We wouldn't leave a man behind, but we would make sure to complete the mission. I knew he'd do whatever it took to get me back out. "I know that too. We're good."

"Truth time? If you go down, I'm getting Anabeth the hell out of Justice. With Camden gone, there just aren't enough trained men around for me to risk her." He grabbed my arm, holding tight. Looking me square in the eye as he said, "And I'll take Katie with me."

Something inside my chest lurched. If anything went wrong, if I ended up in jail, Katie'd have no one to protect her. Bishop knew that...probably better than most because he'd just gotten Anabeth back right in the middle of all this shit. We'd already had to kill to keep his woman safe. Him promising to make sure mine would make it through under his guard? There were no words for how much that meant. Save for five.

"All in, all the time."

He nodded once and let me go. "Let's get this shit done. I want to go home."

Chapter Eleven

KATIE

The kitchen—and therefore, my entire world—wasn't the same without Gage in it. A really weird thing to think about considering he hadn't been in either very much. Not in the grand scheme of things. He hadn't grown up with me or gone to school with me, hadn't worked with me or been my neighbor. He'd simply appeared one day, and since then, he'd always been there.

On second thought, always seemed excessive. He hadn't *always* been there…he'd just spent a lot of time in The Baker's Cottage kitchen and thus with me since I'd opened the place. Lots of very quiet time on his end, making my nerves flare hot and bright as he listened to me babble on about everything and nothing.

Not that he was the only thing making me nervous, because even though he'd left, I couldn't relax. The butterflies I tended to get when around Gage had stayed put in my stomach, my nerves refusing to settle and even growing worse the longer I spent without him. Four days under his constant watch, and I was ruined. Absolutely ruined. The fact that I didn't have that big, burly shadow looking out for me was a reminder that things could go wrong quickly. And then what? What would I do if he wasn't there to fight with me? Not to protect me, really, just...to have my back. And for me to have his. Because things could just as easily go wrong up on that ridge as they could here in town. A thought that didn't do a damn thing to help me relax.

Alder sat on the stool in the corner, my guard in case the Soul Suckers showed up, but his presence didn't instill the same confidence in me as Gage's did. Alder seemed like an excellent protector—tall and mean-looking and altogether scary when he got mad—but he wasn't my wild mountain man. He didn't watch me the way Gage did. In fact, he tended to keep his eyes on Shye. Understandable, and yet...I almost felt like a third wheel in my own kitchen.

But Gage hadn't left me alone with only Alder and Shye. He'd left me with his dog too. Rex had stayed with me throughout the day, keeping tight to my legs and staring at me every time I moved an inch. The dog had done exactly as his owner had told him to—he'd guarded me. And he'd done it with cocked ears, an almost constant tail wag, and a goofy doggy smile on his face. I was seriously beginning to fall in love with Gage's dog. How was he so smart and still so adorable?

"You know, the health department will close me down if they see you." I shook my head when Rex wagged his tail harder and looked up at me. The beast wore such a loving expression, I couldn't deny him. "Yeah, yeah. Just...hide in the back if anyone comes in, okay?"

I tossed him a piece of beef fat from the counter, frowning when he scarfed it down and whimpered for more. I'd already fed him a few times, something I was sure I'd hear about from Gage. But I couldn't tell Rex no when he seemed so sad and hungry.

I was a sucker. "Greedy dog."

Rex scooted closer, still looking up at me, still wagging his tail. Irresistible and completely distracting, just like his owner.

I'd fallen behind that morning because of Gage's tendency to steal all my attention. Not that I would complain out loud about any of it—having a big, bearded, sexy man throw you on a counter and eat your pussy like it was a veritable feast wasn't something to complain about. Especially not when I remembered the feel of his thick fingers inside me, the arousing scratchiness of his beard against my skin. The way his voice deepened and his words seemed to fuel the fire burning with me.

I can't wait for you to ride my face.

Yeah, not a damn thing to complain about except that he'd needed to go into work. I hadn't been able to keep my heart from racing since he'd left, hadn't found my place of calm either. Even the monotony of the tasks I'd done a million times couldn't clear my head. I knew it was because Gage wasn't with me, but still— this was my kitchen, and no biker gang was going to make me feel uncomfortable in it.

Except, as I stared down at my gloved and bandaged hand, I knew that thought was a lie. They'd already made me afraid to be here alone. It was easy with Gage spending all his time with me, but without him? Being out of the safety of his watchful eyes? I just wanted to go home and hide. A fact that made me feel weak and useless.

"Gage is going to kill you," Shye said as she barreled through the doors. Alder grinned and grabbed her arm, tugging her between his spread legs to hold her close. To nuzzle her neck and kiss her collarbone. That was when I looked away—third wheel for sure in a kitchen I no longer felt safe in. Definitely weak.

"He won't kill me. He'll just...be a little mad." Okay, little was an understatement. He'd heard the same instructions from the doctors that I had—no working, rest the hands, easy stretches every day to keep the skin from tightening too much, but that was it.

Yeah. Just like with the dog, I couldn't sit still knowing the people of Justice were hungry and wanted my food. So I'd cooked a few dishes. Nothing too much—a batch of bread from some dough I'd frozen the week before, a chicken and rice soup, along with a beef stew that came together quickly. Just a couple of things to package and sell on a carry-out basis. Nothing too strenuous. My hands barely hurt from the effort. And if my fingers wouldn't straighten all the way because the muscles felt tight, well...I'd work that out later.

Okay, yeah. Gage was going to kill me.

"Let me help you." Alder jumped up, grabbing the empty stock pot I'd been shoving along the counter, too worried about hurting myself more to actually lift it. "Where do you want it?"

"In the sink. I need to rinse it out before I put it in the dishwasher."

"Consider it done." He headed to the sink, Shye smiling after him.

"You are so gone," I said once he was out of earshot, shaking my head. That girl had fallen hard and fast for the former Green Beret. Not that I could blame her. Alder looked at her the way anyone in their right mind would want to be looked at—as if she were both something to eat and someone he'd never get enough of.

Luckily, she seemed to realize how good she had it. "Yeah. I am. Though I have a feeling you're not far behind me."

My face heated, and I—for once—had nothing to say. Obviously, my attraction to Gage Shepherd was strong enough for the little blonde to notice, and I wasn't about to deny that. I just...didn't know what to do about it. Other than let him have his way with me whenever and wherever it pleased him.

Shye laughed and headed back into the dining room, manning the front and selling orders for me. Alder soon followed her, leaving me alone in the kitchen with Rex and my soups. I didn't mind his absence. Not really. At least, not at first. I kept expecting Gage to come through the doors, though. Kept waiting for him.

All day, the anxiety I'd felt at his not being there grew. I hated it—hating feeling so reliant on him. Hated knowing those biker bastards had gotten to me. Hated the fact that, hours after I'd assumed we'd have left, my hands had started to ache horribly and I just wanted to go home to rest.

The restaurant grew quiet as the day passed, the orders for soup and bread tapering off to nothing. I almost had my kitchen clean and back to rights when I finally took a step away from my tasks and looked up. But this time, I wasn't disappointed.

Gage.

He stood in his usual corner, looking unusually rough and grim. And dirty. Filthy, really. Dried mud made his jeans appear awfully stiff, and he had more dirt on his face and hands. My god, the man must have come straight from the job site. Or from burying a body. He looked *that* filthy and lethal in the moment.

I could only think of one thing to say. "You scared me."

I expected a smile, something to acknowledge the reminder of the other night when I'd said the same thing to him. I didn't get it.

"You're not supposed to be working." Even though his words seemed scolding, his voice wrapped around me like a blanket, soothing my frazzled nerves. Calming me quicker than anything else could have.

"People were hungry."

"And you couldn't help but feed them."

My heart pounded heavy in my chest, my attention not on what I'd done at all because he was *here*. "Where've you been?"

That heavy brow came down a little, changing his expression. "Work."

"That's it? Work?" I didn't feel right questioning him that way, and I especially didn't feel right being irritated at such a short answer. I also didn't know what I was doing. I should have run to him, wrapped my arms around his thick neck and stolen every bit of comfort he had to offer me. Instead, I hid behind my prep counter and tried not to think about how much I needed him. How badly the tremors running through me were rocking my body. How much better I would feel if he would just hug me.

And so I started babbling, a bitter tone to my words that even I heard. "Work. Okay, yeah. I knew that. I guess I didn't expect it to take so long, though. I've been here with Alder and Shye. And Rex. Your dog hasn't left my side. He hasn't been outside in hours, though. Alder wouldn't let me take him for a walk, and he didn't feel—"

I nearly screamed when he grabbed me. Without a word, Gage spun me around and bent me back, his arms supporting my weight as he planted a deep, hard kiss on my lips. And oh, was it good. He stole my breath, licking into my mouth and devouring me in a way no man had ever done. Grabbing me tight and holding me as if I might disappear. Making my legs shake and my knees go weak with his lips and tongue and hands. Fuck me, the man had to be the best kisser on the planet. And he was kissing *me*.

A smile danced across his face when he pulled away. "You missed me."

Yes. But that one word refused to come. Instead, I said, "Your dog has eaten me out of house and home."

His grin only grew, as if he knew what I was thinking. "You didn't have to feed him."

"Yeah, well, you try to disappoint that face."

Gage hummed, and he took a step back to lean a hip against the counter. He kept his hands on me, though. Pulled me right between his legs so my body practically rested on his. Thankfully. "Bishop's home for a few days, and we had a job to do out of town. There was a problem on the way back, but it all worked out. That's why it took so long."

"Oh." Rex chose that moment to rub against my legs, giving me the perfect excuse to look away from those dark eyes that saw too much. "I shouldn't have thought—"

"Princess."

"Yeah?"

He pulled me in tighter, resting his hands on my ass. Holding me up. "You can ask me where I've been. If it's not with you, though, it doesn't matter. Because with you is the only place I want to be."

Double oh. My heart jumped, practically diving into my stomach and scattering the butterflies until there was nothing left of them. Peace and calm washed over me, and my nerves finally —*finally*—settled. I sighed at the warmth spreading through me, letting Gage hold me. Letting him wrap me up and keep me in his arms. Melting into his touch the way I'd been wanting to all afternoon.

Gage rubbed my back, his big body relaxing around mine as he held me. As I acquiesced to the need to surrender to this. To *him*. Silently. Too silently, apparently.

"Was that too much?" Gage finally asked, his voice low and deep. Soothing.

I shook my head, breathing him in. "Not at all. I just...wasn't ready."

For him. For this. To feel so needy. To want so much. But I did—I wanted. So, so much.

Gage kissed the top of my head and gave my ass a solid smack. "Well, get ready, Katie Baker, because I'm not going anywhere. Now, give me your phone."

I jerked back, his words—the order to hand over my phone—surprising. "What?"

"Your phone. Give it to me." He smiled all slow and sweet. "Please."

I pulled my phone from my pocket, unsure if I wanted to give it to him. It was just so personal. Most of my life was inside that device. "What are you going to do with it?"

He raised an eyebrow. "Are you afraid I'll see something I won't like?"

"No. I just...it's my phone, and you're being very demanding."

"I said please." He nodded toward the device still clutched in my hand. "Fine—you drive. Unlock it and click your Find Friends app."

Find Friends...the app that let you see where anyone's phone was if they gave you permission. Where you could track down people when they weren't with you. I'd never really used it, not having anyone I'd needed to keep track of. Not wanting anyone to be able to know so much about me either. Still, I did as he said, the pieces of what he was giving me slowly falling into place.

"Pull up my name," he said in that deep voice that sent shivers up my spine. I looked away from the screen, meeting his gaze. His dark eyes held mine, his smile still in place. Relaxed and calm and completely comfortable with his actions. "Add me."

Two words that made my throat dry and my heart race. "But then I'll know where you are."

"Exactly."

"Are you sure? What if you don't want me to know something?"

But Gage never flinched, never faltered. He simply said, "Add me. I'll approve it."

So much confidence. Maybe some people would have seen this move as unimportant or not a big deal, but I didn't. I knew exactly how much trust you needed in order to give someone that much access to your life. I didn't take this lightly.

I clicked add and typed in his name until his contact information came up. Until his name on my screen didn't terrify me. Then I clicked send. "All done."

He grunted as his phone pinged, reaching into his pocket to pull out the device. A few taps and he showed me the face of it. "*Now,* it's done. You can know exactly where I am at all times."

But it didn't feel done—in fact, it felt one-sided. Something I could fix.

Not a nerve in sight, I took his phone from his hand, pulling up the same app and searching for my name in his contacts. Clicking buttons until I'd added myself to his list. Until I gave him the same access he gave to me.

Once done, I handed his phone back to him and went through the steps on my own to approve his request for access to my location. No fear, no anxiety, no butterflies. Just Gage and me and a plethora of satellites keeping us together. "*Now,* it's done— and it's a two-way street. If I can know where you are, you can know where I am."

Gage stared down at me, an unreadable expression on his face. "That's a big step in the trust department."

"It is."

"You sure you're ready for that?"

No fear. "With you, yeah."

He yanked me closer, looking positively fierce and feral. "I don't know how I got so lucky to earn your trust, Katie Baker, but I don't take it lightly. I won't break it."

I loved the sound of a promise on his lips. "I know."

"Good." He brought my hand to his mouth to kiss the back. "What's left for you to do here?"

I ran through the list in my head: a counter to clean, a cutting board to wash, and a knife to put away. "Just a few things to clean, then I can go."

"Okay. Let's get those finished so I can get you home before dark."

"You've been working all day—just relax for a few, and I'll finish up."

"Fine, but don't be afraid to ask for my help. I'm happy to give it." He headed for his stool in the corner with Rex at his side. I should have been able to focus again, to get to work on the last few tasks I needed to finish now that he was back. Instead, Gage stole some of my attention, and when he picked up Rex, he had it all.

He plopped Rex on his lap, snuggling the dog and scratching behind his ears as if he'd missed the beast as much as he'd missed me. Rex curled into his owner's chest, tail wagging faster than I'd ever seen it. Both obviously happy to see one another. Why was that so damn hot?

But watching a man love on his dog wouldn't get the work done, and I really did want to go home. My place, Bishop's… didn't matter. So long as I was with Gage, I'd be happy. I finished wiping down the prep counter and tucking all my tools away, leaving everything perfectly placed for whatever might happen tomorrow. I washed the bread knife and made sure that was back on the magnetic strip where it belonged, too. One last task and we could leave.

I had just picked up the cutting board I'd been using to slice bread—the thick, heavy one made of slats of maple—when my right hand cramped horribly. I yelped and dropped the board, grabbing my hand and tugging it against my chest. Closing my eyes as pain shot all the way up my arm

Gage was beside me in a breath, pulling my arm away from me so he could look. His thick beard couldn't hide his heavy frown. "What happened?"

"Nothing." I shrugged when he gave me an irritated glare. "Just tired, I think. It cramped up."

"Because you did more than you're supposed to. How have your hands been all day?"

I couldn't help but be honest. "They were fine at first, but after the past few hours, they're... Not good."

"You worked too much."

I had...but I didn't regret it. "People came to the restaurant. I had to feed them."

"You served lunch?"

"Sort of. We did bread and soup, carry-out style. Shye did most of the running and selling."

"But you cooked everything." His frown intensified. "Did you talk to anyone?"

That question brought back the nerves I'd already squashed. "Of course. Some of the guys I've known forever worried because the restaurant was closed. Hunter's dad even mentioned he hadn't seen the lights on in my apartment for a few days. Once I told them about the accident and staying with you out at Bishop's, they were fine."

Something close to a worried expression flashed across his

face, disappearing before I could pinpoint the exact emotion. "I'm sorry, princess. I should have been here."

"You had to work." I cringed as another cramp stiffened my hand.

Gage definitely noticed. "Have you taken anything for the pain?"

"No."

"I can fix that." He leaned down to kiss my bandaged palm before heading into my office. He returned with a packet of pain relievers—one probably from the first aid kit I kept in there.

"This will help until we get you home, okay?" His face darkened, eyes growing more worried. More intense. "But we're not staying at Bishop's tonight."

"Where are we going instead?"

His frown deepened. "Someplace a little farther from town. I need to talk to Alder about it before he leaves, but then we'll pack you up and get you out of here. Okay?"

I shrugged. It wasn't like I was going to tell him no. Wasn't like I really had a choice either. Not in a bad way, more in a "I refuse to be separated from him again" way.

Gage seemed to accept that as an answer, turning and heading for the dining room with Rex at his heels. But he wasn't done with me yet. "Hey, princess?"

"Yeah?"

"Before I forget to tell you..." His smile sent tingles on a path from my heart to my pussy and back. "I missed you too."

Chapter Twelve

GAGE

Need. It burned bright inside of me, blazing a path from my groin to my throat. I needed Katie—her presence, her smile, her eyes locked on mine with that happy expression on her pretty face. Needed it. I'd come back from making Rock's death look like an accident to thoughts of getting her the hell out of there. Instead, the second I saw her standing in that kitchen looking sexy and fuckable, I'd become a goddamned beast with one thought on my mind—getting inside that hot, curvy little body. And when she'd admitted to cooking for the town? When she'd told me that people knew where she was staying? That thought had turned from one of lust to one of pure need to protect.

We definitely would not be going back to Bishop's place.

Alder stood in the dining room staring out the front window toward the highway that ran perpendicular to Main Street. You could just make out the intersection, just see any cars that might happen to pass by, though what he was looking for, I didn't know. Something bad, if the intensity of his stare was any indication. Shye sat behind the bar with a book, looking completely calm and patient. And distracted.

"You get everything handled?" he asked, not looking at me. Not asking specifics on purpose. The less anyone knew about what Bishop and I had been doing, the better.

"Absolutely."

"Good. Finn called." Alder said, his eyes still watching the street outside. "The sheriff passed the Jury Room about ten minutes ago."

Which meant he was heading this way. No wonder Alder couldn't look away from the view outside. "You think he's going to stop here?"

"Don't know. You sure you handled shit?"

As in, could the murder be pinned on me. "There's always the unknown, but if he shows, it'd likely not be for me."

"And my brother?"

"Less likely for him."

"Which leaves us with Katie. What's her relationship with him like these days?"

Fuck. Nothing to do but be honest. "He's definitely the one who ordered the kidnapping, but I don't know her side of things."

It wasn't often that someone caught Alder Kennard off guard, but apparently, I just had. "What do you mean, you don't know?"

"We haven't talked about him."

"You planning on it?"

Not yet, but soon. "Of course."

"Good, because I don't like surprises. He's in bed with the Soul Suckers, and we need to know how close Katie is with him so we can figure out how to handle her."

He wouldn't be *handling* her at all, but I understood what he meant. Didn't like it, but understood it. Any relationship between her and her uncle made us all more vulnerable to the Soul Suckers, especially Katie. A fact I wasn't unaware of. "I'll take care of it."

Alder nodded, still watching the outside world with stiff shoulders and a parade-rest stance. Waiting. Ready to fight if needed. "The Soul Suckers are going to come back for us. For Katie." He paused, his voice dropping lower as he nearly whispered, "For my Shye."

Definitely. A thought that made me want to destroy them before they got close to us. But Alder ran the show in town, so the decision to attack or not rested on his shoulders. "What do you want to do about it?"

He didn't speak for a long moment, still staring out the window. Scowling as the sheriff's cruiser flew by the end of Main Street along the highway at a speed well over the limit. Not stopping, not even looking, but making a point nonetheless. There was nothing we could do to keep him out of Justice. At least, not while he wore that badge on his chest. And breathed.

Alder relaxed slightly when the cruiser disappeared into the distance. "I'm sick and tired of this cat-and-mouse thing—they come in, they hit us, they run and hide. Meanwhile, we sit here and wait for the next attack and hope it's not as bad as the night Leah..."

I didn't need him to finish that statement. We hoped nothing ended up as bad as the night Leah had died in a fire set by the Soul Suckers. They'd tried—with Shye, with Anabeth, and recently, with Katie. We'd blocked all those attempts, but that didn't mean shit. Luck ran out, and even the best-trained men and women lost sometimes.

I wasn't losing Katie. "Every time they come back, they get a little bolder."

"And every time they come back, the damage gets a little worse. But we haven't lost another person on our side, so I guess I have to take that as a win." He shook his head, finally tearing his eyes away from the street outside. "What do you think?"

"I think it's time to act," I said, not holding back now that he'd asked. Going all in, SEAL style. "I think the sheriff wants Katie for some reason, and I don't think he'll stop just because the crew who tried didn't succeed. I think he's also getting and passing on information about us and the people in this town to the Soul Suckers. He's an asset in their pocket, one that gives them an advantage." Balls to the wall time. "We need to level the playing field."

If my comment surprised him, he didn't show it. "And how do you think we should do that?"

My plan, my girl, my problem to face. "I'll handle it."

His gaze pinned me in place, his eyes hard. "That's a hell of a hornet's nest to stir up. You got thoughts on how you're going to do that without blowback?"

"Not yet, but I'm working on it."

"Well, you keep working on it until you're sure, then you bring that plan to Deacon and me. I'm not watching another of my brothers get locked up."

My throat tightened, those words setting me back on my heels as nothing else could have. Bishop had been like a brother to me for years, and I considered the guys in Justice practically family. Alder calling me brother meant there was no *practically*. "I won't fuck it up."

"I know you won't." He turned away from the window, eyes darting to Shye as if checking on her before returning to me. "What's your immediate plan? I can't imagine you left Katie in the kitchen just to shoot the shit with me."

He was right about that. There was a hazel-eyed beauty in the kitchen who was in danger, and I would do anything to keep her safe. Even if that meant running.

"I'm getting Katie out of town."

"I figured that would be coming." He nodded, returning his stare to the world outside the restaurant. "I'd get Shye out of here as well, except..."

Except he had a business to run in Justice. Except the responsibility of being a Kennard didn't end when shit got tough. Except he couldn't abandon the town.

Neither could I.

"Where are you headed?"

"My cabin in the valley." I caught the surprise flash across his face as he turned my way. "No one knows about it but Bishop and you guys, so I think it'll be safer."

"I figured you'd be going farther. Leave Justice behind."

"I won't abandon my brothers," I said, making sure every word came with weight attached. With meaning. "We live together, work together, and fight together. But I need people here to think Katie's gone. I need them to believe she isn't anywhere near Justice so I have time to figure out a plan."

Alder grunted before turning away from the windows altogether. "What's your strategy?"

"I take Katie to my cabin and hide out for a few days. You spread the word that we're down in Colorado Springs to see a doctor."

"I can do that. Old Vol's wife will spread that gossip far and wide if I get it to her."

That took me by surprise. "Vol's wife is a gossip?"

"Vol's wife is *the* gossip. She means well, but she loves to be the one person in the room with information. Likes the attention, I think. I'll make sure she knows you two are gone, and she'll tell every man and woman she sees." His brow dropped down over his blue stare. "Are you thinking someone's selling us out to the Soul Suckers?"

"No, not directly."

"But words travel."

"Exactly. And fake ones go as far as real ones."

"I'll make sure they do. You take care of that girl. I let her come back, gave her this building so she could get started. I feel real fucking responsible that she's now a target for all this."

"This isn't on you. I don't see it that way, and I'm sure Katie doesn't either." I reached out, bumping his fist with mine. "I'm going to change my clothes and wash up in the restroom, then we're headed out. I want her tucked away before the sun goes down tonight. Text me if you need anything. And tell Bishop not to go back to his house. He should stay at Anabeth's for a few days."

"Something we need to know?"

"Katie talked to a few people today and mentioned staying at Bishop's with me. I don't want anything meant for us to head his way."

Alder nodded. "Good call. I'll call him and make sure they're somewhere else."

I was halfway to the kitchen when his rough voice called me back. "Gage."

"Yeah, boss?"

This time, he didn't mince words. Didn't break eye contact either. His gaze held mine, heavy and fierce. Protective. "Watch your back up there."

I could only nod, knowing there was nothing to say. I'd be watching my back for sure. And Katie's. I had to.

Chapter Thirteen

GAGE

My stomach churned and my throat felt tight as I pulled up to my cabin that night. Not Bishop's place, not Katie's. Mine. The one I wanted to share with her. The one I planned to finish building and get right *for her*. It wasn't right yet. There was no kitchen, no paint, no furniture for the living areas. But there was a bed, and we'd brought things like towels and toiletries. I even had food from the restaurant in a cooler. It might not be perfect just yet, but it would do for a hideout.

"Why are we staying here?" Katie asked as I parked the truck under a towering pine tree that would eventually shade my driveway. *Our* driveway. Shit, I was getting so far ahead of myself. One step at a time—set up trust, build a relationship, destroy the Soul Suckers, kill her uncle, make her mine. I couldn't just jump ahead.

"I need a favor."

My phone vibrated against my leg, stealing my attention. I snatched it up, having been waiting on a message from Alder. The text message contained only four words—*plan is in motion.*

Vol's wife thought Katie and I were in Colorado Springs, and she'd start spreading that story to anyone who'd listen. Good.

I tucked the phone away and gave her what I hoped was a reassuring smile. "Sorry. I was expecting a text from Alder."

Her hazel eyes shone bright in the golden light of the sunset around us. "Everything all right?"

"Everything will be." Not quite yet, though, because I didn't have her naked. Didn't have her in my bed and underneath me. I knew we needed to talk, that I needed to figure out everything between her uncle and her, but being in the car with her for the past forty-five minutes—her curvy little body pressed up against mine as she sat in the middle seat—had knocked my brain for a loop. We could talk later—there were things for us to do first.

"C'mon, Rex." I opened my door, the dog slipping across the floorboard to hop down. Katie waited for me, then slid the rest of the way across the seat to exit on my side. I wanted to be a gentleman and help her down, but my thoughts were anything but gentlemanly.

Like right then, with her hand resting in mine and her tits bouncing when she landed on the ground. I couldn't help but wonder what it would feel like to have her hands all over me, to hang on to those breasts with both hands as I rode her hard and deep. My lips practically ached to kiss her, but I wouldn't stop at kissing her mouth. Hell no. I'd lick and suck on every part of her I could. I wanted to suckle her so bad, wanted her taste and smell all over me. Wanted to redden her skin with my beard before soothing it with my tongue. All of that hit me as her little body came to rest beside mine, so close I could practically feel her body heat. The animal inside of me wanted to pick her up, press her against the truck, and fuck her right there in the driveway. But I would be a gentleman, at least on the outside.

"What sort of favor do you need?" Katie looked up at me, so trusting. So perfect. All those dirty thoughts turned warmer, sweeter, just like her. I wanted to pump her full of my cock and simply hold her on the couch. Wanted to smack her ass and watch it jiggle as I pounded into her from behind and sit with her in my lap as she told me about her day. Being away from her that afternoon had been torture, and I'd done everything I could to get back to her as soon as possible. Not soon enough, though, because her hands hurt her. She'd done too much. Maybe I shouldn't ask her for more.

"How are your hands?"

She shrugged, letting me lead her to the front door. "Fine. The painkillers worked. Gage, what favor do you need?"

I held the door open for Katie and Rex, keeping an eye on her as she took in the construction site that was hopefully our future home. Wondering if she liked the vaulted ceiling and the openness of the space. The smoky, beetle kill pine floors I'd picked out with the warm tone that would look amazing against her bare skin. No walls blocked the views of the living area—I hadn't wanted anything standing between me and the reason I'd bought the place. The view.

I'd ripped out the back wall and replaced it with almost all glass, giving anyone inside the house a perfect view of the mountains and forest out back. The view beyond the kitchen— Mother Nature's stunning artistry—painted the most beautiful backdrop.

Not as beautiful as Katie when she saw it, though. Her mouth fell open, and she stepped forward, almost seeming to be pulled by the vista beyond the glass. "This is..."

She didn't have to finish her statement for me to know what

she meant. "Yeah. It is. That view of the far side of Widow's Ridge is why I bought this place."

"I wondered. I mean...you mentioned that you had a cabin you were remodeling, but this is a little farther from town than I would have expected. I couldn't figure out why you wanted to be this far out."

"Do you understand now?"

She nodded, the movement slow and reverent. "The view is worth the extra time to get here."

Exactly. I wrapped my arms around her from behind, pulling her against my chest. Staring more at her reflection than the world outside. "I'm glad you think so, because I love this place. I love having you here, too."

Her smile appeared unbidden, her cheeks flushing a soft pink. "No kitchen, though. You brought a chef home with you, and you have no kitchen. I'm surprised."

I loved when she got that teasing tone in her voice. "The kitchen's next on the list. You can help me plan out what to do with the space. I think I have the base cabinets' plan pretty well set, but I have to finish plotting out where all the wall cabinets go. Then I can get them all ordered."

She hummed, melting into my hold. "I wouldn't bother with wall cabinets at all."

"No?"

"No. I'd put shelves on that wall"—she pointed to the side where I'd planned to create a big bank of cabinets almost like a pantry—"with cabinets under them, but the rest? One big island. It's not a perfect working triangle, but I wouldn't want to block a single angle of this view. Taking a few extra steps here and there would be worth it."

Done. "I'll make sure that happens."

She turned in my arms, smiling up at me. Looking almost patronizing. "Your house, your kitchen. You do what *you* want."

What I wanted was to make a home with her here, but I doubted she was ready for that declaration yet, so I held back. Just like I did when I saw a little flash of pink against her lips. Her tongue—fuck, what I wanted her to do with that. But not yet.

"So," she said, drawing the word out. "What's this favor you need from me?"

I ran a hand over my beard and into my hair. "I need a trim."

"Why?"

"Because you said I needed one."

Her eyes grew huge. "I...I didn't mean—"

I kissed her. How could I not? She seemed so flustered at the idea that I'd paid attention to what she'd said. As if I'd ever ignore her words. Every syllable meant something, even when she got nervous and shot a thousand of them at me in under a minute. Of course I took them to heart.

When I finally pulled my mouth from hers, I cupped her face and kept her close. Giving her my honesty. "There's no one in town to do it, and I probably won't make it to Rock Falls for a while. You want me to trim my hair and beard? Done—I'll do anything to make you happy, and if one of those things means you might find me more attractive? That's a no-brainer. Finding a place to actually get it done...that's not as easy."

"I don't want you to do something you don't want to," she said, her voice barely more than a whisper. My silly girl.

"Katie, this?" I tugged on my beard. "This is nothing. If you'd be more comfortable with me not having it—"

"No." She blushed darker, licking her lips again. "Don't... shave it off. I like the beard."

I knew women had a thing for beards. "Just not this much."

"Just not that much."

"So help me fix it. I want to look attractive for you."

"Not for me."

"Nobody else matters." I told Rex to stay, ignoring the irritated huff he gave me at being relegated to his living room bed, and dragged Katie behind me to the master bedroom. Most of the work in there was done—it just needed painting and a couple of small hardware pieces added to the en suite bath. I'd moved a few boxes over already, figuring I should have some stuff for the nights I worked on the construction too late to head back to Bishop's. My forethought would come in handy. After shutting the door to make sure Rex didn't chase after us, I dug through a box in the closet until I found what I was looking for.

"You own clippers?" Katie asked, eyes on the Wahl case in my hand.

"Of course. Just because I don't trim my beard often doesn't mean I'm not prepared to."

I smacked her ass as I walked past her, loving the way it jiggled. Loving the way she squeaked and blushed even more. This might be fun. I grabbed the small step stool that had been hidden in the corner since I'd installed the shower head and set that up in the middle of the bathroom. I could look in the mirror from that spot, but Katie could still move all around me. Perfect. Once I had the basics ready, I grabbed a towel from under the sink and settled in.

"Ready."

She looked at the clippers, frowning. "You're really okay with me doing this?"

"Yup."

"I might screw it up."

"I went ten years with a buzz cut for the military. I can always go back to that if I need to."

She hummed, staring down at me. Good goddamn, did she look amazing in my bathroom. She stood behind me, so I only got her reflection in the mirrors, but she fit. With me, in this space, the one I'd built. She *fit*.

Katie started slow, using the hand scissors to cut the longer pieces before grabbing the clippers for the sides. She took her time, staring down at me. Frowning and concentrating. Silent, too. Focused, like when she cooked, just not mumbling to herself. I didn't even know if she realized she did that—talked to herself when she got really into the job at hand. It had taken me a couple of days to figure it out, to understand the words she said when she was in that zone. Directions. Instructions. Likely the lessons pounded into her head through cooking school. She whispered them as she worked. She didn't whisper as she trimmed my hair.

She did seem thoughtful, though. "So, if you're willing to trim it, why do you let it get so long in the first place?"

"It seemed to fit the place." I caught her eyes in the mirror. "I'm from a suburb outside of Detroit—lots of businessmen in suits or slacks and collared shirts, you know? But I'd head south of the city to where a lot of the factory workers lived, and there'd be these men with big beards and long hair who hunted and fished and seemed to make a lot of trouble. I spent ten years in the SEALs following the rules and wearing the old high and tight haircut—when I got out, I wanted to live more like those men south of Detroit instead of the suits I'd grown up with."

"So you moved to Justice and wanted to make trouble?"

"Definitely. But only the good kind." Her grin warmed me right in the chest. Fuck, I was gone over this girl.

"Have you been making a lot of trouble since you've been here?" Katie asked, suddenly sounding a little more nervous than I'd like. I had no clue why, though.

"Depends on what you mean by trouble. What are you asking, princess?"

Her face flushed a little. "Nothing really. I just...I don't know what you do usually. When you're not stuck babysitting me."

Oh hell no. I tugged her closer, pulling her between my legs and making sure I was in her face. "This isn't babysitting, Katie. It's me making sure you're safe. I would have done that for anyone in town, but I'm real fucking happy it's you because I've wanted to get you alone for a long time. As for what I usually do —I work. I fix this place up. I train Rex. And if there was a spare minute in the past few months, I tried to figure out how to spend time with you without making you nervous. That's it."

She ran her hand over my cheek. "Seems lonely."

Fuck yeah, it had been at times. "Bishop and Rex kept me entertained. What about you? Other than the restaurant, I don't know what you do."

"The restaurant is *all* I do. It's been my true focus since I moved home."

"No friends? Family in the area?" That sounded rehearsed, which hadn't been my intention. I needed to know to formulate a plan, but I didn't want to pump her for information. There was a line between the two that I needed to find—and soon.

Katie simply shrugged. "I hang out with Shye at work—she's nice. Mercy Bell and I have run into each other a few times in the hallway, but we're not really close or anything. The rest of the people in town—they're all friendly, but they still see me as little Katie, poor, practically orphaned daughter of Mac. Did you know my dad died logging for the Kennards?"

"I'd heard something about that."

"Yeah, so...I love them all, but they'll never not think of him when they see me. It's a big shadow to live under."

She didn't mention her uncle, and I didn't push. Not yet.

"Seems lonely."

She gave me a quick smile. "Not so much anymore."

I loved that answer, so I let her go. Let her get back to the business of cutting my hair and beard so she could finish. I watched her instead of myself, keeping my eyes locked on the way her body moved around me. How she didn't take her eyes off me as she worked. So when she stepped back after shaving down my neck, I was sort of surprised by what I saw in the mirror.

She'd left everything longer than I would have expected.

"Is it okay?" she asked, looking so damn nervous. I couldn't have that. I pulled her between my legs and dragged her down until I could steal a kiss from those soft, pink lips of hers. Licked my way inside and tasted her deeply, groaning when she fisted my hair and tugged me closer.

"Is it okay for you?" I asked when I finally let her go.

She nodded, running her fingers through the long waves on top of my head. The sides she'd trimmed down short, not military tight but way neater than I normally wore them. The top stayed long, and my beard was still full and thick. Just...not so bushy. I didn't know how she did it. Or why.

"I figured you'd have gone shorter."

She smiled, her fingers moving from my hair down the side of my face. "I like you a little wild."

Then I'd always be wild for her. I leaned into her touch, practically fucking purring as she stroked me. Wanting so much more of her touch. Too hungry for it to hold off any longer. To hold back.

I grabbed her hips and yanked her closer, rubbing my face against her chest. Teasing her nipples through her shirt. "Do you have any idea how much I think about your tits?"

Her laugh rumbled through her chest. "None whatsoever,

though I'm not surprised. Men have been obsessed with them since they came in when I was in middle school."

I growled as I looked up at her, holding her gaze while I bit down on her nipple through her shirt. Breathing hard against her to tease her with a little heat. "I would have beat their asses if I'd been here."

"No, you wouldn't have. I was such a dorky kid back then. The only thing I had going for me was my breasts."

"Somehow I doubt that."

"It's the truth. I was quiet and sort of shy, and everyone knew my dad had been the logger who'd died on the job, so they all treated me differently. It was a weird way to grow up. Plus, I had zero confidence."

"None?"

"None." She huffed, frowning, her eyes unfocused. "Guess that comes from always being told how fat you are."

The fuck she said? "Excuse me?"

She waved her hand as if it was nothing, but it was obviously something. The hurt in her eyes didn't lie. "My mom was an exercise junkie. She wanted to eat healthy and stay young forever, you know? That...wreaked a little havoc on my teenage self."

"Is that why you cook? Because of your mom?"

She snorted a sarcastic laugh. "Yeah, but not like you think. Her idea of a good dinner was cutting open a box of something so she could know exactly how many calories were in it. When the cancer took her, I was convinced it was because of all those processed foods."

I thought about her menu, her kitchen, the food she made with such care, the worry on her face as she'd inspected every box of produce that morning. "You don't cook with processed stuff."

Her eyes met mine, wide and shocked. "Right. I don't like it."

"That's why you offered to make me healthier granola bars."

She nodded, still looking surprised. As if I didn't pay attention to her or something. With a sigh, she pulled me in closer, fisting my hair and tugging. Sending sparks of desire shooting down my spine.

"If eating the way I had to as a child taught me anything, it was that you should be able to pronounce everything that goes in your mouth."

Fuck, she smelled so good. Felt good, too. I was far too distracted by that to deal with words. We could talk about her mom another day. Right then, I needed her.

I grabbed her ass, rubbing. Bending down to lick along her waistband. "I can pronounce pussy."

"Gage."

"Is cunt better? Because I can pronounce both. I'd also happily eat your pussy or cunt right now if you wanted me to."

Her breath caught, and her eyes locked on mine. "You already did that today."

Yeah, I had. But it hadn't been enough. I'd never get enough.

"I'd do it every day, multiple times a day, if you let me." I slid my hand down her thigh, coming back up between them. Teasing her. "I'd happily eat at the House of Katie for every single meal."

"You're ridiculous." She moved as if to pull away, but I wasn't done with her. Hell, I hadn't even started with her yet. So I pulled her close, yanking her across my lap. Gripping and tugging until she straddled me right there on the step stool.

"I'm not ridiculous, Katie. I'm hungry for you." Then I kissed her, slicking my tongue past her lips and owning her mouth. Tasting her as she began that slow, sensual writhe that meant I had her. And I planned on keeping her, pushing her until she broke. Making her come with my name on her lips.

She jerked when I dug my fingers into her fleshy thighs, bumping against where I was already hard for her. My cock ached so badly, and the tip felt wet with precome. Every roll of her hips over mine, every little groan or grunt as I pressed against her, only made it worse. I wanted to fuck her, to bury myself deep inside her sweet heaven and never come back out.

And I fully intended to do so. As soon as I got her in my bed.

Chapter Fourteen

KATIE

This man killed me.

Not in a bad way—not like the Soul Suckers seemed to want to do. Gage Shepherd killed me with his dark eyes and the heat they held when he looked at me. He killed me with his sweetness, such a surprise considering his gruff exterior. He killed me with his kisses and his hands and his hard cock wedged between us. I wanted to die a little death right there on his lap in the bathroom, but he had other plans.

With his mouth still owning mine, he stood, taking me with him. Carrying me through the bathroom and into the bedroom as if I weighed nothing. His hands gripped my thighs so tight, so strong. Left me wishing I was already naked so I could feel his rough skin against mine. So intense, so damn manly. Nothing like the men I'd dated before, and yet I couldn't get enough of him. Couldn't see ever wanting a man who was less than what he gave me.

Gage laid me on the mattress all sweet and gentle-like, following me down, never letting go as he settled over me. And then he was on me—his weight pressing me deeper into the bed. His thighs nudging my legs apart so he could lie between them. So he could notch himself against my hips and join us from chest to feet.

And, oh god, his cock.

So hard and big, it pressed against where I was already so wet for him. I could feel the heat there, practically taste the need pulsing through his body the same way it did through mine. I'd never wanted my clothes gone so badly. I craved skin-on-skin contact with all of him—every hard and soft inch, every inch of him that could possibly touch an inch of me. All of it. The wildness and the sweetness, the troublemaker and the man who followed orders. I just wanted Gage. And though I'd tamed him a little—not much considering how much harder I could have gone after him with the clippers—I couldn't stand the thought of taking more from him than I had. Didn't want to. I liked him wild. I wanted him to make me wild.

"Gage," I murmured when he finally—*finally*—freed my mouth so he could suck and lick a path down my neck. "Please."

"What do you want, princess? What do you need?"

His voice pulled a shiver from my body, his words hot against my neck. "You. Just you."

"Oh, you have me." He pulled back, rocking his hips against mine as he braced himself on his arms, his muscles tense, locked like steel cables. Practically caging me in. "C'mon, princess. I want to hear you ask for it. Tell me what you want."

I couldn't find the words. All I wanted, all I needed, was him inside me. But I couldn't say that for some reason. Couldn't beg him to fuck me. I'd never been very vocal during sex, never really had a reason to be, I guessed. But, with Gage? I wanted to be. I just didn't know how.

He seemed to sense that, or maybe my silence lasted too long. He dropped down to kiss me again, still rolling his hips against mine. Still teasing me with one hell of a dry hump as he pressed his cock right against my pussy and made me moan and writhe beneath him.

"You know what I want, princess? Want to know what I've dreamed about doing to you these past few months?" He groaned at my nod. "I've been dying to get a taste of that sweet pussy. Now that I have, I fucking crave it. But there's more. There's always been more. I've wanted to know how hot and wet you get when I tease that little clit. I've wanted to know exactly how deep I can fuck you before you can't take another inch. I want to feel your pussy clench on my cock as you come, and I want to taste you afterward to know if your cunt gets sweeter when you're all swollen and sated."

"Jesus, Gage." I arched under him, wanting the same things. Wanting to feel him inside of me. For him to fill me. "Please. I want all that. Please."

And thank the heavens, the man conceded. He rolled to the side, stripping me of my clothes in seconds as I worked on his jeans. As I stared at the slow reveal of his heavy cock. So thick and long and red, the tip nearly purple. There was nothing gentle about it, nothing that gave me a moment's peace or made me relax. His cock matched the rest of him—primitive and brutal, and I still wanted every inch.

"I love the way you're staring at my cock, princess. You look so hungry for it."

I leaned over him, forcing him onto his back and catching his eye before opening my mouth over him. Arranging myself so my face was even with his hips. I didn't take him inside, though.

Nothing so blatant. Instead, I licked that blunt, ruddy tip. Teased the slit with my tongue before swirling it around the head. Tasting him. He grunted and bucked his hips when I finally took the entire head in my mouth, his hands gripping my shoulders. Holding on to me. Stopping me.

"Not yet, Katie. Fuck, I want you to suck me so bad, but not yet."

He dragged me up the length of him then rolled me over, pinning me to the mattress once more as he stole my mouth with his. Naked and wrapped around one another, just as I wanted us to be. All that skin-on-skin contact was exactly what I needed.

His cock lay trapped between us, rubbing against my pussy and teasing my entrance as he circled his hips on mine. As he teased me like the troublemaker I knew him to be. I arched and twisted and tried to bring him inside me, but he kept his hips locked in place, kept his mouth on mine and his hands gripping me tight. Kept me completely at his mercy.

I couldn't stand it but loved every second, too.

"Gage."

He groaned, moving down my neck. Sliding his body along mine as he headed south with his mouth dragging along my flesh. And, oh god, his tongue. He teased me with it, licking and kissing and nibbling his way along my collarbone and to my breasts. Sucking hard on my nipples as he held my hands at my sides. Popping off to come back to them, making me gasp and arch and beg for more while he held me down. Not letting me move. Not letting me touch. Controlling me completely.

"Please," I nearly whimpered as he dragged his beard along my stomach.

"That was a mean little trick you pulled, teasing me with that hot little tongue the way you did. You think I'm too noble not to fuck that mouth of yours? Because I'm not. Not even close," he said, sliding lower until I could feel his breath across where I was so damn wet for him. "But I wasn't kidding when I said I craved the taste of your pussy. And I know I got a good fill earlier today, but I need it again. Need you on my tongue before I fuck you, princess. I want it so bad."

He pulled my legs up higher as he settled his shoulders between them, spreading me wide open for him. I should have been embarrassed, should have felt too exposed or something. I didn't, though. Not with Gage. There was no need to feel shy around him, especially not when he stared down at me in what I could only call reverence and licked his lips.

"Look at this pretty cunt dripping for me." Gage groaned, rubbing his face against my thigh and letting his nose trail along my opening. "I'm going to eat you so good, princess. I'm going to fuck you with my tongue and get you all soft and wet—more than you already are—so I can fill you with my cock later. I just have to get a taste first, have to know this sweet pussy's all broken in and ready for me."

The man never said what he didn't mean. He tasted me, though tasted was really the wrong word. Too weak, too bland. Gage *devoured* me. He showed no mercy, pulling my lips apart as he closed his lips around my clit and sucked. As he dove right in and went at my clit in the most direct way possible. I nearly exploded off the bed, my free hand grabbing his hair and tugging him against me. Not wanting him to stop. Not wanting to miss a second of his brutal attack. He grunted and obeyed, inching closer, hanging onto my hips with a grip just this side of painful and pulling my pussy to his mouth. Not letting me get away from him for a second. I doubted he ever would—at least not until he had me sated and wrung out. Until he had me as wet and swollen as he wanted me to be. And then he'd fuck me.

I had no idea how I was going to survive it.

My first orgasm slammed into me without warning, coming hard and fast as he lashed my clit with his tongue. I screamed his name as I came, every inch of me shaking. Every sense pared down until it was only him and me and that moment. His mouth on my pussy, his hands holding my thighs so my legs draped over his shoulders, his beard making everything more sensitive. I screamed and bowed and clung to him as my entire body shook with my release.

That didn't stop Gage, though. He gripped my thighs tighter, mumbling something about sweet and luscious and fucking incredible as he continued torturing me with his tongue. As he chased me up the bed, his thick body moving mine with ease, until he had me pressed against the headboard as my second orgasm rocked through me. Until I was pushing him off me, too sensitive to let him keep assaulting my clit. Too wet and wanting to wait another minute.

"Now, Gage," I said, gasping. "Now."

Gage grunted and grabbed my hips, dragging me back down the mattress before sliding up my body. Covering me once more. Laying his weight on me as I caught my breath.

"So fucking sweet." Gage kissed me deeply, letting me taste myself on his lips before pulling away again. "I'll never get enough of tasting your cunt, princess."

And I would never get enough of him making me feel the way I did right then—beautiful and languid but still so turned on and desperate for him. I wrapped my legs around his hips, squeezing him closer. Wanting him so bad, I almost couldn't find the words.

Almost.

"I want you inside me. I want to feel all of you."

He groaned, stretching to the side to grab a condom from the pocket of his jeans. He tore open the foil packet with his teeth, then reached down to sheath his cock before lining us up. One hand under my thigh, pulling my leg up, spreading me for him again. The other arm braced against the mattress, supporting his weight. Leaving enough room between us for his chest hair to tease my nipples in a way that made me want so much more. Made me feel empty and needful again. Ready for everything from him.

"Gage—"

"Anything you want," he whispered against my lips as he nudged his way inside me. "I'll give you anything. Give you everything. Just stay with me, princess. I'll take care of you."

And then he was there, pressing inside, stretching me with his girth and length and, oh god, it felt so good. So, so good. I must have said that out loud because he nodded, hissing a yes before rolling his hips into mine. Pressing harder as my pussy gave way for him. Giving me more. Fucking me slow and easy and deep. So very deep.

"Fuck, Katie. You're so damn wet and soft. How are you so soft?" Gage lifted his upper body from mine, rolling every muscle in waves as he kept thrusting deep. As he teased and pressed and filled me to the brink. As he finally bottomed out, his hips all the way against mine, his cock completely buried inside of me. I couldn't hold still beneath him, couldn't stand not to move as the pleasure-pain of that big cock invading my body overrode every other sensation possible. I writhed, pinned down by his hips, only one hand able to reach for him. To grab at his shoulders and scratch into his flesh. To hang on as my mind spiraled out of control.

"Gage. Damn it." I bit my lip and tossed my head back as he thrust harder, smacking his hips into mine. Filling me right to the edge of pain. To the edge of *more*. So much more.

"You going to come on my cock, princess? Should I tease you a little more? Is that what you need?"

My groan was my only response as he released my hand and moved his arm between us so he could press his thumb against my clit. Pressure. Nothing but Gage and sex and pressure. That had become my world, my life. My present. I fell into the rhythm of his thrusts, twisting my hips to meet his. Lifting my knees so he could slide deeper, fill me more. So he could drive me right back over the same edge with his cock that he already had with his tongue.

And he did.

I came so hard, there was no room for anything else. Not for words or thoughts or senses. It was only me and the pleasure ripping through me, screaming along my nerve endings and turning my body into a live wire. At least, that was all there was until the energy started to fade. That was when I heard Gage mumbling the filthiest fucking words against my ear as he slammed into me faster than before. Words about my cunt, how tight I was, how good I felt around his cock. How wet I'd become. How much he wanted to lick up every drop. How he wanted to claim me with his cock. How badly he wanted to fill me with his come and watch it run down my thighs afterward.

Fuck, I wanted that too. Wanted it badly—to know he was there, inside me, owning my body the way only he could. Wanted the reminder later, that feeling of wetness to tell me this wasn't a dream. That I really had fucked Gage Shepherd, that he'd come inside me and marked me as his. Base, dirty, and wrong—but I still wanted it. Wanted to be his in every way.

"Fuck, can't hold back." He moaned, hips hitting harder and faster, his rhythm stuttering as he lost his grip on his control. As he gave himself over to his needs.

As I dug my fingers into the back of his neck and pulled his face to mine, unable to hold back. Unable not to say the words swimming inside my head. "Come inside me, Gage. I want to see you lose control all because my pussy feels so good wrapped around your thick cock. Come for me so I never have to question if I'm yours."

Gage groaned a sound that was loud and guttural, pressing deep and shivering all over as he came. As he buried himself deep and swelled inside of me. But before he was done, before he finished coming, he dove in for a soul-shattering kiss. One that spoke of power and control, of need and desire. Of fucking lust and want and carnal pleasure taken to the max. He kissed me as if he'd never get a chance to do it again, still bucking and twitching inside of me. Still getting off. And I took it. Took everything he had to give me as I tried to make my body obey my mind so I could wrap myself around him and clench hard on his cock. So I could make it better for him. So I could bring him the same pleasure he had brought me.

So I could be enough to deserve a man like Gage Shepherd.

"Goddamn, Katie," he said, grunting slightly as he collapsed on top of me. I loved the feeling of him covering me, loved the heaviness of him. I could have stayed that way for hours, but Gage would never trap me underneath him that way. He rose onto his elbows, keeping his forehead against my chest but relieving the majority of his weight. He didn't pull out of me immediately. Instead, he lay on top of me, breathing hard. Still filling me.

I trailed my fingers up his spine, grinning when he shivered. "So I guess that means it was good, yeah?"

His chuckle rolled through his body, and he lifted his head. "Good isn't nearly the right words for what that was." He leaned in to kiss me all sweet and soft before rolling away. "Don't move."

I didn't. Instead, I watched as he got up to dispose of the condom and wash his hands. Then he was back, walking toward me as if totally comfortable in his flesh. As if being naked was nothing to him. And maybe it wasn't. I felt no need to cover up either once I saw the heat in his eyes as he looked me over, as he dragged that dark gaze over my naked flesh from head to toe. If I looked at him with half as much want and appreciation, then I could understand his brazenness.

He climbed back onto the bed and lay down beside me, rolling me into his arms so we were facing each other. So he held me against his chest with our legs tangled together. Soft and slow, he dragged his fingers up my back. Soothing me. Leaning in to place soft, sweet kisses against my lips. Ones that made me feel things, good things. Romantic, long-term things. Feelings I'd never experienced before. I'd never expected him to be so gentle, especially not after the way he fucked me, but I liked it. I'd take that kind of affection any day. I'd take all of him.

Hopefully, he wanted to take all of me, too.

Chapter Fifteen

GAGE

I woke up Katie twice that night—once with my mouth latched on to her pussy and once with my fingers buried inside her. Both times ended with me balls deep and her coming on my cock, so if she minded me pulling her from sleep, she didn't show it. In fact, if the happy sighs and the way she clung to me were any indication, she didn't mind a bit.

The third time I woke up wasn't so pleasurable.

I couldn't have said what pulled me from sleep just before dawn. A noise, a feeling, a sense of something off. A disturbance of some sort, for sure, just nothing distinct. And nothing big enough to wake my princess. Katie slept peacefully, her head on my chest and her one leg hitched up over my hip. As I lay in the dark, feeling her weight on me, I had a quick thought of going for round three—of seeing if I could actually have my cock inside her before she woke up—but something about the way I'd woken up felt off.

My cock would *not* override my instincts, which were screaming at me to get up. To investigate. To protect.

Instead of rolling my girl underneath me, I carefully slid from her hold and crept out of bed. I pulled on my jeans as quietly as possible, grabbed my gun from the nightstand, then headed for the living room. Rex stood just outside the bedroom door, his ears up, his back straight, and a low growl rumbling in his throat. Looked like I wasn't the only one who thought something felt off.

The two of us moved through the dark house, sticking to the deepest shadows until we made it to the front door. Everything seemed right—house secure and quiet. Looking outside, everything again seemed fine. There was nothing but darkness blanketing the hillside, the sky to the east just barely lightening with the coming dawn. But as I'd learned early on in my career with the SEALs, everything could seem fine and go straight to shit in about two-point-five seconds. I needed to go out there.

I hated leaving Katie alone, but I couldn't ignore this, couldn't pretend Rex wasn't hearing something out there as well. But instead of rushing outside, I waited, letting my eyes adjust to the low light. Giving myself time to get my bearings before cracking open the front door. Rex came with me, sticking right to my side, silent just like me. On guard and prepared for just about anything.

Once across the porch, I tucked myself into a corner and waited, listening, watching the tree line as the sky began to glow. Sticking to the shadows again to hide myself away. Off to the west, a crashing sound came from the woods. Too loud to be a human unless it was a really stupid human. I couldn't count that possibility out, but I had a feeling it was something other than a dumbass human. More than likely, a bear had gotten a little too close to my house—that was probably what Rex sensed and I heard. Probably.

I hated not knowing for sure.

About ten minutes after the sky turned a deep golden red color, after the sun finally peeked over the treetops, a pulsing sort of growl broke the stillness of the morning. A bear threatening something out in the woods. Perhaps another bear had moved too close to a food source, or a mother was warning off something she saw as a danger to her cub. They'd be fattening themselves up this time of year, readying themselves to spend the winter in their dens hibernating. Hearing them thrashing through the woods in search of food or fighting off other animals wasn't unusual or something to worry about.

Didn't stop me from worrying, though.

But after another ten minutes without hearing or seeing anything to make me think the bears weren't the most dangerous things in these woods, I figured it was okay to relax. A little.

"Stand down," I whispered, waiting for Rex to follow my order before stepping out of the corner. I kept my gun up, kept it aimed into the woods. Just in case. And yet, nothing. No sign of anything wrong, no sense of anyone watching me. So I signaled to Rex to follow me back inside. Just a bear. Definitely a bear.

But as I stood in the bedroom looking over a sleeping Katie, I couldn't rid myself of the feeling that something was wrong. It was likely the noise of the bear outside that had woken me or the sound of Rex growling. Nothing more. And yet...

Yeah, there was no fucking way I was falling asleep again, no matter how inviting Katie's warm body tangled up in my sheets was.

I headed out to the living room, thinking about coffee and noises and how many guns I had in the house. Not enough, that was for sure. I'd brought my jump bag and some extra ammunition with me, even a few small grenades to make a statement if I needed to. It didn't feel like I was ready, though. Something I wasn't used to. I didn't normally worry about being unprepared, but I'd never had someone as special to protect. I'd never had something as important as Katie to lose.

Every bit of my unease came from having her with me. Not *her*, really, but the knowledge that I needed to keep her safe. That her life was in my hands. That I still needed to get information from her, but that I'd waited too damn long and now would need to deal with the fact that I'd likely piss her off when I told her about her uncle. Katie didn't trust me completely—her nervousness around me had made that clear. I'd been careful with her, not pushing, but holding back would likely come around to bite me in the ass. Me not telling her what I knew about her uncle would likely be seen as a breach of that fragile trust between us.

Fuck, I couldn't even think about what that would bring. The thought of her being mad, of her possibly walking away, made my lungs feel tight.

I needed a distraction. One that didn't involve my dick.

I grabbed my phone and pulled up my messaging app instead of waking Katie again. I needed to check in with Bishop, make sure he and Anabeth were settled. I sent him a quick note telling him to give me a call when he got up and hoping Anabeth was feeling better, then I pulled up Deacon's name. He'd been on a date—a second date—a few days back, and I hadn't heard how it went. Not that we needed to gossip about details, but if he was starting up something with Felicia, my personal meteorologist, I'd make sure to back off on my daily texts to her.

Surprisingly, ten seconds after I sent off a *How'd the date go?* message, my phone rang.

"Good morning, sunshine," Deacon said when I accepted his call.

"What the fuck are you doing up so early?"

"I could ask you the same thing. Alder said you were taking Katie to your cabin for a few days. I figured you'd be too busy to even think about your old friend Deacon."

"I am. Way too busy. But Rex started licking his asshole, and that made me think of you. So here we are."

Deacon laughed, making me smile in return. "What's really up, kid? You can't have trouble, or you wouldn't be busting my balls."

"I can multitask. Honestly, though, I'm awake and thought I'd check in on you and Bishop. Make sure everything was good."

"I'm cool. I heard Bishop's been home with Anabeth—I guess she hasn't been feeling too well, so he's in protective man-bear mode."

"Protective man-bear? You need to get out more."

"I have been."

He sounded damn near chipper. "With Felicia?"

"Yeah. Got two more dates under me."

Fuck. There went my personalized weather reports. "Good news, man. Glad that's working out for you."

"Don't get ahead of yourself there. It's just a few dates."

Sure it was. I'd never known the man to talk about a woman before, so I had a feeling it was more than the casual fling he seemed to want me to think it was. Not that I was going to push him.

"No getting ahead of myself. Seriously, though. What are you doing up so early?"

"I own a bar, Gage. I haven't gone to bed yet."

"Right. That place." That actually made sense. I sat on the floor, my back to a wall, my long legs crossed at the ankles in front of me. Too tired to stand or walk. Keeping an eye on Rex as he paced in the kitchen. His focus stayed outside, on the woods, as the sun brightened the world outside. The bears would be heading back to their dens already, so that shouldn't be bothering the dog. Or maybe they'd gotten into more of a fight than I was aware of, and he was responding to that. Or maybe the dog was getting old. "C'mere, Rex."

"What about you?" Deacon asked just as Rex ran for me and crawled into my lap. "What's got your panties in a twist before seven in the morning."

The fear that someone would take Katie away from me, or that she'd just fucking leave on her own. I ran a hand over Rex's scruff, using him to keep from worrying down a path not yet needed. "Heard something outside. Adrenaline is a bitch."

Deacon's teasing tone dropped immediately. "You all good up there?"

"Yeah. Seemed to be a bear."

"Seemed to be or was?"

Hard question to answer. "There's nothing to say it wasn't just a bear I heard—damn thing was tromping through the woods looking for a fight."

"But..."

Yeah. *That.* "But I had a bad feeling, that's all."

"You need backup?"

"Not yet."

"Well, call me if you do. And you two can come stay with me if you need another set of eyes on Katie."

Fuck, my Justice brothers were the best. "You keep your eyes off my girl, old man."

Another laugh from Deacon. "You afraid of a little competition?"

"There'd be no competition. I'd win by default."

"Cocky."

"That's what she said."

His snorted laugh was about all I could expect in response to that one. "All right, man. I think I'm going to make some coffee and get my day started. You should get some sleep. You're too old for these late hours."

"And you can fuck right off, sir. Good night."

He hung up without waiting for my response, always needing the last word. I was okay with that, though. I didn't need a last word; I just needed Katie safe. Something that was growing increasingly more difficult, at least in my head. I sat on the floor, petting Rex, for a good long time. Seeking a path through the brambles I'd created. Trying to figure out the best way to handle everything. Unable to see the forest for the trees, as they said.

Eventually, I rose from the floor, made a pot of coffee, and stared out at Widow's Ridge as the sun turned the trees a thousand different shades of gold and green. I thought about how to go about getting Katie to talk about her family without giving myself away, pinning down a small plan as I drank my first cup of wake-up juice. It would be sneaky, not being up front with her, but I'd deal with that when I needed to. Katie's safety came first.

It would always come first.

<h1 style="text-align:center">Chapter Sixteen</h1>

KATIE

My body ached in the best way the next morning. Hours of sex interspersed with snuggling and sleeping had left me exhausted but happy. Satisfied, even. But seriously…so tired.

Gage had woken me up twice overnight—had fucked me good both times, too. His mouth, his hands, his cock. All of him had worshiped my pussy until I'd been a big, incoherent ball of sensation without thought or purpose. I could only feel, only experience all he did to my body. And it had been amazing.

But the morning had come, the sun lightening the room to the point where I could no longer deny my need to get up. I wasn't one to stay in bed and lollygag or sleep in, usually. I probably would have stayed in bed if Gage had been in there with me. If his warm body had been pressed against mine, his hands on my skin and his mouth at my neck. Sadly, I was alone in his big bed. Gage wasn't even in the room, something I found odd and maybe just a little hurtful. I would have thought he'd have wanted to stay with me that morning, or that he'd have woken me when he got up. Not even in a sexual way, but just to say good morning and start the day together. Instead, he had left me to wake up alone.

My happy bubble wobbled pretty damn hard at that.

Still, I was nothing if not resilient. I rolled out of bed and stumbled toward the bathroom. No time to worry about things that were likely not as big of a deal in reality as they were in my head. So he was already up—maybe Rex needed to go out, or Gage needed to investigate something. I could be an adult and not assume the world was falling on my head because of one morning waking up alone.

Still...odd.

After a quick bathroom trip, I headed out to the great room. Gage stood next to a folding table pushed up against a wall, a corded cooktop in front of him and a mug in his hand. Barefoot —shirtless—wearing dark jeans that hung loose enough to show off his stomach and the dark line of hair leading under the waistband. My knees shook, and a spark of desire shot through me. He looked so damn handsome, especially with his new, neatened hair and beard. I hadn't wanted to change him too much, but our time with the clippers had done wonders. Still wild, rough around the edges for sure, but the trim made him a little neater and more polished. From a grizzly mountain man to a fuckhot one with the deepest, darkest eyes I'd ever seen and a smile that could melt a woman's panties in less than a second.

He was also as chatty as an old bear in the morning, apparently.

Gage grunted when he saw me, holding up a second mug in invitation. Coffee. I could use it. His eyes stayed on me, dragging down my body and back up as I slipped closer. He didn't need to tell me he liked the way I looked wearing one of his shirts—it was right there in the expression on his face. In the fire burning behind the darkness of his eyes. The man had my nipples tight with nothing more than a good eye-fuck—and I liked it.

But as I took the mug from him, the butterflies in my stomach started dancing again. I had no idea what to say to him. *Thanks for last night...want to go again...does this mean you'll call me later?* Oh my god, what if he didn't want to call me later? I had his number, but I'd never used it for personal messages or anything. Could I now? Was I supposed to? How could I ask for it after last night? How could I not? We were basically living together, though... Would there be any calling involved?

My stomach turned faster, my throat tightening, until I couldn't hold back a second longer. "So, I've been thinking about making pasties. Not here, but at the restaurant. When I officially open again. I had them one time when I went on a trip to the Upper Peninsula of Michigan—have you ever been there?—anyway, they're like meat pies or stew sandwiches. I need to figure out the right recipe for the dough, though. The stews I already make..."

Words tumbled out of my mouth, completely unstoppable. And all the while, he watched me, his face slowly pulling down into a deep frown that only made me want to talk more, get the words out faster, to distract him from whatever upset him. I didn't even stop when he set his mug down and grabbed mine to do the same, leaving me to flap my hands around as if I needed the motions to match the words.

"Some people put butter on them or even jelly, though that level of sweetness isn't really the right flavor profile for the treats." *Flap, flap, flap.* "I could make a fruit salsa maybe to go with them, but old Vol would probably still slather his in grape jelly like a kid at—"

Gage grabbed me around the hips and yanked me closer,

pressing his mouth to mine in a kiss that tasted of coffee and him and everything hot about the night before. I melted into him, kissing him back, stroking his tongue with mine as his hand slid down to grab my ass. As he gripped and tugged and demanded. I loved it when he did that.

"Good morning," he murmured against my lips before diving in for another kiss. Another deep one that seemed to last and last and last. That slowed down and turned more sensual than rough, more asking than demanding. That had me trembling in his arms as my entire body went languid.

The man could *kiss*.

Eventually, though, he pulled away, looking down at me with hooded, dark eyes. "What's got you so worked up today?"

Him. Always him. Which I couldn't say. Instead, I clung to his shirt, ducking my head against his chest. Almost afraid to look into his eyes and see...well, not what I wanted to see. "Last night... I don't know what to think. I mean, I don't want to make up things in my head or assume we're on the same page and we haven't talked about anything yet, so maybe I'm jumping the gun—"

He kissed me again, groaning softly as he kneaded the flesh of my ass and pulled me tightly into his hold. Good lord, the man broke me with every kiss. One press of his lips and I forgot every care and concern I'd ever had. One slip of his tongue against mine and I was ready for whatever he wanted to give me. And the beard —I'd never been with a man with a beard before, but I liked it. The hair was softer than I'd expected it to be, and the tickle it left when he moved to kiss and suck down the length of my neck had me shivering against him.

"Gage," I whispered, wanting so badly to go back to bed. We didn't, though. Instead, Gage hummed a little and ended the kiss again, rocking me slightly as he held my gaze.

"First things first, princess. You can jump my gun anytime you like." His chuckle matched mine, and the fact that he didn't let me go—that he held me close as he rubbed my back—soothed a lot of my nerves. "Second, I like action more than talk. Always have. So what I don't say, I'll show." He nuzzled my neck, keeping his hands on my ass and groaning. "And hopefully, I'm showing you that I can't get enough of you, princess, so don't you worry about anything with me. I wouldn't have started something I wasn't intending to finish. Third, would you like some breakfast?"

I don't think my eyes had ever been so wide. "You're going to cook for me?"

He nodded, watching me with a small smile playing on his lips.

"But...no one ever cooks for me. They always expect me to do it."

"Because you're a chef."

"Yeah."

"Well, you're off duty right now." He glanced at his hot plate and pans, frowning. "I can't promise you my eggs will be as good as ones you make, but they'll be hot."

"Hot is good."

He looked me up and down again, teasing my thigh at the edge of his shirt with his fingertips. Leaning close so he could whisper against my lips, "Hot is damn good."

Soaked. I was already soaked for him. But he wanted to cook me breakfast, and I wanted to let him. So I pulled away. "I should go get dressed."

He patted my ass and gave me a quick, smacking kiss on the lips. "Go ahead. And feel free to grab anything you need from my bathroom or closet. Especially the closet. I like the idea of you wearing my clothes."

I shot a look down to his jeans, eyeing the impressive bulge there. "I can tell."

His laugh followed me down the hall and back into the bedroom. I brushed my hair and tied it into a messy bun. I had lip gloss and powder in my bag, but nothing else. Nothing to make me feel pretty or put together. So instead, I worked with what I knew Gage liked—I kept his shirt on, tying it at the waist so it didn't fall to my knees. Not perfect, but it'd do. I also slipped into a pair of his boxer shorts. I had to roll the waist a few times, but they'd keep me covered. I skipped the bra and panties I'd packed for the night. Might have been wishful thinking on my part, but I was okay with that.

I was feeling a hopeful sort of buoyancy as I walked into the great room. At least, until I came face-to-face with Gage's gun. Not that he pointed it at me, more that it was *right there*. On the table. Laying next to the carton of eggs as if it was totally normal to cook breakfast with a handgun beside you.

Totally not normal.

I gripped my right hand with my left, rubbing. Trying to ease the slight ache in the muscles as that gun stared back at me. As every second of *that* night came back to overtake my thoughts. The kiss in the gym, the fear of knowing someone was looking for me, the terror of that guy Rock pointing Gage's gun at him. I'd thought I was going to die—and that gun reminded me of all of it.

"Hey. Can you grab—"

Gage didn't finish his question. I looked up to find him staring at me, his face flat and almost emotionless, no fire behind those eyes like earlier. On guard, it seemed. It was a swift kick in the ass to remind me that this man was a soldier—a fighter. He'd been a Navy SEAL, which meant he'd likely seen some serious action overseas. I knew that, had always known it, but seeing it right there in front of me? Knowing how comfortable he was with his gun, while it did nothing but instill terror in me? That was hard to come to grips with.

With his brow furrowed as if trying to solve a puzzle, he looked at my hands, at where I was still rubbing my right with my left, then at his gun, then back to my face. I could almost see the puzzle pieces fitting together in his mind, and for once, I had no idea what to say to him. There were simply no words for this situation.

Gage turned away, his movements quick and precise as he plated the eggs and turned off his cooktop. He grabbed a couple of slices of toast from the little toaster tucked against the wall and set them on the plates as well before wiping his hands on a towel. And then he faced me again. Slowly, like a man approaching a wounded animal, he slipped closer. Coming for me. My breath sped up, my chest tightening with every step he took. My world narrowing down to only him.

When he reached me, he took my right hand in his, flipping it palm-side up. Staring down at the ugly burn. He ran two fingers over the worst of it—the part that had nearly been third degree—then leaned in to place a soft, gentle kiss there. "I'm so sorry for this."

Oh. That...wasn't what I'd expected. "It wasn't your fault."

"It was. You're mine to protect, and I failed." He kissed my palm again, looking into my eyes as he promised, "They'll never lay another finger on you."

I believed him. "I know."

"Do you? Because that gun there is part of protecting you. I can see how nervous it makes you, but it's necessary."

Protecting me. Everything seemed to be about Gage protecting me. Who was protecting him?

"What about the other one? The gun Rock stole from you."

His jaw tensed, his teeth grinding for just a moment before he said, "I'll take care of it."

And though I hated the idea of him going up against Rock again, I knew his words were true. He'd take care of it...he'd take care of everything.

———

The eggs weren't perfect—I liked mine finished with a little crème fraîche and fresh herbs—but just as Gage had promised, they were hot. And yummy. He'd cooked them in a little butter, whisking them until they were super fluffy before pouring them in the warmed pan. Not that it mattered. The eggs could have been a hard, rubbery mess and I still would have enjoyed the meal because it came with Gage.

Breakfast was amazing.

"I can wash the dishes," I said as Gage rose from the little card table he'd set up for us to eat at. He gave me a look that had me sitting deeper in my chair. "Or not."

"Your hands are still healing, so we'll go with not. Besides, I don't have a kitchen sink—these are going to be scraped and rinsed in the bathroom for now."

True on all counts. Gage disappeared down the hall, dishes in hand. I waited for him to come back, spotting how neat everything still was. Orderly. Gage definitely liked a clean environment around him. Even Rex—who lay in his bed across the room—always seemed clean and neat. Only Gage's wild man hair and beard had broken the pattern of control. Not so much anymore, though.

I shot him a smile when he came back into the living room, freshly rinsed plates in hand. "So you cook and you clean up. Someone taught you right."

God, I hoped it wasn't another woman.

Gage shook his head with a grin, oblivious to my sudden angst. "My mom made sure her son could take care of himself before he left the house. That son being me. And whatever she didn't teach me, the military did."

I practically snorted, grateful the other woman in his life had at least been related to him. "You're luckier than I was, then. The only thing my mom taught me about cooking was how to read the directions on a box."

Gage's shoulders seemed to stiffen, his back straighter than before. "You mentioned that once. She was a health nut, right?"

If only. "Not quite. More...she was always thinking that her problems in life came down to how she looked. Specifically, to the little pooch her belly developed after she had me. Once my dad died, it became an obsession for her. She used to tell me if she could just lose a few more pounds, the men would notice her, and then everything would be okay. That's where the need to diet and exercise came from."

"Doesn't seem like a good plan."

"It wasn't. She never lost those last few pounds, and all that processed food rotted her gut. At least, I believe it did. She died of colon cancer a few years back."

"I'm sorry."

I shrugged, missing her like always. Fighting back the ache that came whenever I let myself remember she was gone. "I miss her. I don't think she would have liked that I've moved back to Justice, though."

"Why not?"

What to tell him? Some secrets carried too much shame to blurt out in the light of day. Some, too much hurt. Mine held both, so I'd have to keep things vague.

"There were problems when I was in high school. Not with the people in Justice, but...others."

Gage's face went flat, emotionless. "Problems."

Not a question, so I didn't answer it. Gage didn't seem to like my non-response.

"What sort of problems and with whom?"

"Did you just use whom correctly?"

"Don't change the subject."

Damn. "I told you I was dorky in high school but I had big breasts."

"I remember that." He didn't glance down at my chest, something that earned him points with me.

"Well, some people thought they could...take advantage of those two things. That they could take from me because they saw me as weak and without friends."

"What kind of taking are we talking about?"

I hadn't thought about that moment in years, that day in a car that should have been a safe place for me. That betrayal. "My clothes were still on when I punched him in the balls and ran, if that helps at all."

"Someone touched you."

I couldn't answer him, could only nod. My mouth had gone too dry to form words.

Gage looked ready to kill someone. "But you got away?"

Another nod and a hard swallow to loosen my tongue. "Then I told my mom."

"And?"

I couldn't even look at him. "And we moved. Left Justice and headed to Denver to get away from the threat."

"She didn't report this guy?"

I wanted to laugh at that. Not in a funny way, more sarcastic. Reporting him hadn't been an option. "No. We ran instead."

After a long silence, Gage said just one word. "Who?"

His voice gave nothing away, so I looked up, expecting pity. Expecting him to feel sorry for me. Instead, he looked ready to kill. Even his words sounded like knives hitting flesh—pounding and sharp. A stab to the air around us.

"Who put their hands on you?"

"No one important." Not to me, at least. It'd been a lot of years since that day, and I wasn't going back down that road just to enact some misguided revenge. There was no point.

Gage let out a huge sigh and cracked his neck, still looking livid. Still making me want to both run away from him and run toward him. Danger and safety all in one handsome package. And when he caught my stare, when he narrowed his eyes and frowned, he looked even more deadly. "Do you have other family?"

A loaded question, and one I answered carefully. "My mother's brother is still around. He's the county sheriff."

A slow head nod in response was what I got. "Sheriff Baker. He's your mom's brother?"

Because of the name thing. "Yeah. She changed our surnames to her maiden one after my dad died. He was a Gaines."

"Katie Gaines." His lips kicked up into a smile. "I like it."

"Me too." Loved it, really. Had always wanted to go back to it but had never taken the time to figure out how to do that. Maybe I could make that a project to research. How to change my name. "But the Gaines' Cottage doesn't have as nice of a ring to it."

"True. You two close?"

My mind seemed to be stuck on the Gaines loop. "Who two?"

"You and your uncle."

Oh. Right. "No. And he's not my uncle."

"But he's your mother's—"

"Yeah. Hers. Her family. Not mine."

Gage grunted. "You don't like him?"

"Not at all."

"That seems to be a common feeling in these parts." Gage sighed and pushed off the wall, coming for me, his eyes playful but intense. "Who touched you all those years ago?"

No way was I answering that. "Why do you want to know?"

He shrugged, yanking my chair out from the table and dropping to his knees before me. Filling up all my visual space with his mass. "Maybe I want to teach him a lesson."

I trembled when he grabbed my knees and dug his fingers into the flesh of my thighs, sensing what was coming. Wanting it. Craving it. "What kind of lesson?"

"The kind that hurts a little bit." He leaned in, biting my inner thigh hard enough to make me jump even as he kept his eyes locked on mine. "The kind that tells him a real man doesn't have to force a woman to do anything. Spread your legs for me, princess."

I did. No questions asked, though his shirt fell between them, keeping two thin layers of fabric between us. Covering me just enough to make me feel like a tease.

Enough to make him groan. "That's my good girl. Forcing you to do something won't get you good and wet for me. It won't have you making those sexy little mewling sounds I love so much. I don't ever want you to think you can't tell me no, okay?"

I nodded, unable to speak. Unable to even catch my breath.

"Look at you all breathless and quaking. You want me to tease you, don't you? Want my hands on that pussy you're hiding from me...or is it my mouth you're craving?"

Both. Everything. All of it.

"Gage." I grabbed his hair, trying to hold him still. To pull him closer. To do...*something*.

Gage dropped closer, dragging his nose along my inner thigh. "Tell me his name, and I'll teach him how a real man is the one who belongs on his knees for his woman."

He was so close to where I wanted him. Close enough for me to feel his breath against my hip as I said, "He's not worth it."

"He hurt you. He scared you. That's not nothing, princess." Gage looked up, his eyes fiery as they met mine. "That's why you came back, isn't it? You wanted to feel safe, and Justice is your safe place."

Only if you called the eye of a hurricane a safe space, but he wasn't far off. I came back because I'd missed feeling taken care of. This town may not have been the safest place for me, but I'd never felt more at home than when I'd lived in Justice. And no one was taking that away from me. So I nodded, unable to deny the entire statement. Remembering the need to go home that had swept over me after my mom had passed.

It'd taken me over a year to trust I was strong enough to risk it, but I'd finally reached a point where I couldn't deny the call any longer. On the anniversary of my mother's death, I'd called Alder and was on the road back to Justice the day after that. It had been a rash decision, one fueled by sadness and grief, but as I sat in Gage's cabin in the woods with the man himself kneeling between my legs, I knew it'd been the right one.

And yet... "I don't always feel safe here."

He didn't know the depth of my fear or what exactly I meant by that, but he still reacted. Still dragged me closer and promised me what he could. "I'll protect you, Katie. Every minute, okay? Nobody gets to touch what's mine."

That word struck home the way nothing else could, freezing my heart and sending a shiver up my spine. *Mine*. Jesus, I wanted that. The security of knowing he would always take care of me, the comfort of having the freedom to do the same for him. I wanted it so badly, I couldn't help but ask, "Am I really yours?"

"Yes." He pulled my legs toward him, forcing me to slouch. Opening me even wider as he wedged himself between my thighs.

"And does that mean you're mine?"

His face. It froze as if he hadn't thought about that, and then a smile spread bright and bold. He looked like a man who'd just been given a gift, a treasure. And somewhere, deep down, I knew that treasure was me.

"Abso-fucking-lutely. I'll always be yours, Katie. Never doubt that."

My heart took off, pounding hard as he rose up on his knees and kissed me. As he sealed that oath between us. His hands gripped my thighs, his shoulders pushing me back until he had me caged. Pinned. Trapped. Not in a scary way, though. This was my Gage, showing me how much he wanted me. How much he needed me. I knew he'd back off in a second if I told him to, but I wanted him that way. A little wild, a little demanding, and a hell of a lot sexy. Giving myself to him was exactly what I needed.

"Hey, Gage?" I asked against his lips, refusing to completely break our kiss.

Thankfully, he seemed just as resistant to the idea of separating. He replied in between kisses, his lips brushing mine with every syllable. "Yeah, princess?"

I spread my legs a little wider and sat back. "I'm not wearing any panties."

He groaned, diving down to run his nose along my inner thigh as he tugged his shirt up my belly. I lifted my legs and placed my heels on the seat of my chair, spreading myself for him. Giving him room. Knowing what he wanted. What I wanted from him.

He gripped my thighs, teasing me with his fingers. "Are you wet for me?"

Easy answer to that one. "Yes."

"How wet? Are you soaking my boxers there, princess?"

"Maybe. Why don't you find out?"

He shot me a sexy little smirk before yanking the boxers down my legs. In the next second, he had my knees over his shoulders and his face absolutely buried in my pussy. And me? I fisted his hair and held on. Knowing this ride would be a wild one.

Chapter Seventeen

GAGE

We spent the day wrapped up in one another. In my bed, on the floor, up against the glass looking out across the ridge—a personal favorite of mine and, if I judged by the way Katie had gone wild on my cock as I'd pinned her against the windows, the same for her. All in all, the day had gone exactly as I'd always hoped it could.

The evening? Well...I should have known that would go to shit.

The temperature outside had dropped significantly as the sun had gone down, and I'd have bet anything there was snow on the horizon for us. Early for the season, but not unheard of in these parts.

Coming in off the back deck, I hurriedly closed the door behind me and tucked my gun into my hip holster. I'd taken Rex outside for a quick perimeter sweep before the sun set completely, not wanting to leave Katie alone once night fell. Too many bad things could creep up on you in the dark forests of the Rockies, including humans with ill intentions. Katie had said something about needing to find a new recipe, so I'd hooked her up with my laptop and tucked her into the bed to work. I was hoping I'd find her there still—a little pre-dinner tumble in the sheets sounded like the perfect plan to warm me back up after spending time in the icy wind.

But as I made the turn from the hallway to the bedroom, I knew sex wasn't in the cards.

"What's wrong?"

Katie sat stiff as a board, her face pale and her eyes wide as she stared at my computer screen. "You already knew about him."

"Who?"

She looked up, those hazel eyes filled with something close to anger. Closer to hurt, actually. Something that scraped along the walls of my chest and made me want to roar into the night at whoever had upset her.

Which, apparently, was me.

"My mom's brother," she said, practically spitting the words at me. Throwing knives with every syllable. "Mark Baker. *Sheriff* Baker. You knew everything already when you asked me about him."

Fuck. I always deleted my search history, so she hadn't seen anything there. But something—I'd left behind something, some trail to my research. Some proof of what I'd done. I hadn't considered she'd find any of that, thought I'd covered my tracks well enough. Apparently, I'd been wrong. "I did, but I—"

"But you pretended like you didn't. You lied to me."

"I didn't lie intentionally. I just wanted *you* to tell me about him instead of making assumptions and guesses."

"You made an assumption thinking it would be okay with me to research—" she looked down at the laptop and ran her finger over the trackpad "—his work history, his current salary, the houses he's owned, other family." She closed the laptop lid, shaking her head. Looking ready to cry. "You knew he was my mom's brother, not my dad's. And you knew I was a Gaines."

There was no way to explain the depth of my guilt at the look on her face. "Katie, I didn't—"

"You did." She tossed my laptop to the side and jumped out of bed. "You absolutely did. You looked into my mom's brother without telling me. You researched *me* and *my life* because of that. And you never said a word about it. Do you know how creepy that is? You looked up everything but know nothing. Everything you found is garbage."

I grabbed her arm as she tried to run past me. "Stop. Creepy? I never meant it to be, I never meant to look into your life at all. We needed information on your uncle—"

"He's not my uncle." She tugged her arm from my hand, pushing her way into the hallway. "All you had to do was ask me, Gage. If you wanted to know that sort of bullshit about Mark, you could have asked me. You didn't need to lie to me."

"Katie, I didn't lie to you. I just...didn't tell you."

"You're still not!" She spun, hands raised in the air and voice growing loud. "Why were you looking into him? What did you find out? And why didn't you tell me anything, with all the time we've spent together?"

"Katie, I didn't want to—"

"Tell me. Right. You don't seem to want to tell me anything."

That was bullshit. "What do you want me to tell you? That Mark Baker is crooked as fuck? The whole damn town knows that. You want me to tell you he's in the Soul Suckers' pockets? Because that's a rumor too. Or do you want to know that he ordered your kidnapping at the restaurant?"

She blinked, her face growing pale. "He what?"

Balls to the wall time. "They knew you'd be there, Katie. Those guys who broke in didn't do it randomly. They had intel on your schedule. They even knew you were there because of a soup."

She started to pace, not looking at me. Not really looking at anything. I could practically see the cogs turning in her head, the pieces of the last week fitting together.

"Because it was gumbo night," she said, her voice barely over a whisper.

"Right."

She shook her head, pacing faster. Eating up space along the windows and looping back again. "He wouldn't have sent someone to try to kill me. He doesn't want me dead."

"He sent them to take you. I know you don't want to believe me, but I'm telling you the truth. Your uncle—"

"He's not my uncle." Her words pounded like fists, hitting hard and violent. Slamming across the space. My head spun, those hits not making sense.

"But he's your mom's brother."

"Exactly. My mom's brother." Eyes like stone, she snarled my way. "Not my uncle."

"I don't get it."

"You don't need to." She wrapped her arms around herself, looking so small and fragile and yet...fierce. Angry. This wasn't a kitten with her claws out—this was the queen of the jungle defending herself. "You betrayed me."

That cut deep, leaving what felt like gaping holes in my chest. "I was only trying to keep you safe."

"By lying to me. So my body could be safe but not my heart." She pushed past me again, heading for the bedroom this time. Back the way we'd come.

I chased after her. "I never lied."

"You did...by omission, but still a lie. Jesus, Gage, I thought you were actually interested to learn stuff about me."

"I was. I *am*."

"Bullshit." She rushed into the room, grabbing her jeans and tugging them on. Looking like a woman about to make a run for it. "You think I can't take care of myself? That I'm so helpless, I have to have you hulking around or else bad things will happen to me? Bad things have already happened, Gage, long before you ever even showed up in this town. And I survived. I made it through them. I'm not some weak little girl who's too afraid of her own shadow—"

She stopped, took a deep breath. Shook her head as if to clear it, to reorganize her thoughts. I had no idea what just happened—what had made her go down that road—but I knew a tangent when I saw one. She hadn't been talking about me, about us, about what I'd done. She'd been focused on something else. *Bad things have already happened*—things I wasn't around to protect her from. Fuck, what had I missed with her?

But before I could ask, before I could figure out how to make her tell me everything bad so I could see if there was a way for me to repair the damage other people had wrought, she stabbed me right in the heart. "I think it's time for me to go home."

"No." My answer exploded out of me, unstoppable and immediate. She was running, and I... No. I couldn't let her. So I set myself in front of the door as I told her, "You're not going anywhere."

And apparently, that was really, really wrong.

"*No?*" she said, her voice deadly cool and calm. Too calm. Dangerously so. "You're going to stand there and tell me no, that I can't leave? Do I not have the right to go when I choose to?" She stepped closer, fury burning hot and bright in her gaze. "Are you just as bad as the Soul Suckers, Gage Shepherd? Have I been kidnapped?"

Her words ripped out something inside of me, leaving an empty sort of burn that hadn't been there before. That hurt like a motherfucker and made it hard for me to breathe. "I'm not like them."

"Then let me go."

No. I wanted so badly to tell her no, but I couldn't. "You won't be safe at your apartment."

"Then I'll call Alder and see what he thinks I should do." She pushed past me, refusing to look me in the eye. Running away from me. "I don't want to stay here anymore."

"Katie." I reached for her, grabbing her elbow out of instinct more than anything. How could I let her walk away? How could I let her put herself in danger? I couldn't, but she was going to anyway.

She yanked her arm away from me, turning to give me a glare that froze me in my tracks. "Don't touch me."

That's when reality stabbed me in the neck. I was behaving just like the Soul Suckers and that guy she'd told me about. The one who'd touched her when she hadn't wanted him to. Demanding her time and attention, not letting her make her own decisions. I'd completely screwed the pooch on this one, and the only way forward was to back up. To retreat. Something I was loath to do but knew I needed to.

"Okay, princess," I said, putting my hands up as if she had a gun on me. Unsurprising—this girl was deadlier than any weapon ever made. She could obliterate me with nothing more than a word, nothing more than a simple *bye*. I'd be destroyed if she left me, so I needed to be cautious. "I won't touch. I won't keep you here either. Please stop for a second and listen to me, though."

Emotionless, her hazel eyes looked past me. "I'm done listening to you."

She was down the hall and heading toward the door in seconds. Before I could even force my feet to respond. Before I could start my heart pumping again. Leaving. She was *leaving*.

Once I wrapped my head around that fact, I hurried after her, desperate to get her to stay. Or to convince her to take me with her. Anything, really, so long as it ended with us in the same place. But she didn't stop on her path to her escape, only paused long enough to grab the keys to my truck from where they sat on the windowsill before pulling the front door open.

Before taking that first step to walk out of my life.

My heart wanted to pour out of my body and onto the floor, but something stopped it. Something caught my attention and made every bit of my military training rush to the forefront. It was nothing, really. A tiny dot. One single spot of red on Katie's shirt that shouldn't have been there. Most people would have overlooked it, but I'd seen that light before. I knew what that was, and it didn't belong on Katie. Not anywhere near her.

A laser sight. Someone had a gun aimed at my girl.

"Katie, down." I was running before I had the words out, watching in slow motion as she turned toward me. Still mad. Still so damned furious with me. Not that it mattered in the moment. She could be angry with me for the rest of my life as long as hers didn't end right there in my entryway.

I hit her just in time, jumping in front of her body and shoving her back into the house as the shot rang out loud and sharp. Whoever was out there wasn't concerned about being caught because there was no sound suppressor on that weapon. They were also awfully close.

Pain ripped through my shoulder as we fell, causing flashbacks of that day I'd been shot. Of Bishop lying on the ground in a puddle of blood. Of the fear that I'd messed up, that I hadn't been quick enough. That I'd lost my best friend because I simply hadn't been *enough*.

But I hadn't lost Bishop that day, and no way was I going to lose Katie now.

As soon as we hit the floor, I put a plan in motion. Jumped up and dragged her farther into the house as I kept my body in front of hers. Trying to cover her from what I knew would be coming through the door any second. To keep me between her and whoever had just shot at us.

Shot her, apparently, because there was blood on the floor. A lot of it. Panic unlike any I'd ever felt flooded me.

"Fuck. I'm sorry, Katie." I worked my hands over her body, trying to find the shot. The hole. The damage. I tried hard, but I was suddenly so tired and my shoulder burned as if it was on fire. Fuck, where had she been hit? I could help her if I found it... could save her if I could stop the bleeding. But my eyes wouldn't focus right, and my right arm wouldn't do what I needed it to. "I'm so sorry. Let me help you."

"You're sorry?" Katie slapped me away, pushing back and sliding along the floor to get out from under me. To get away from me, it seemed. I tried to pull her back against me, but she only fought harder. "Gage, stop. You're bleeding."

It took a second for her words to make sense. I was the one bleeding? That meant she wasn't shot—I was. Oh, thank Christ for small miracles. I'd taken the bullet, not her. Not my princess. She wasn't going to bleed out all over the floor. That didn't mean she was safe, though.

"We need to move," I said, trying hard to keep my focus off the incredible pain in my shoulder. Yeah, that felt like a gunshot wound, all right. And if we didn't get out of the path of whoever had fired on us, there would be more.

I kicked the door closed behind me and sat up, pushing myself back and leaning against it. Blocking anyone's way in. Roadblock in human form. It took me three tries to pull my phone from my pocket because my right arm simply couldn't move the way I needed it to and I'd already grabbed my gun with my left. I wasn't setting the fucker down again either. Left may not be my normal firing hand, but it would have to do.

"Gage, stop moving around," Katie said, looking as if she wanted to pull me away from the door and drag me into the living room. As if she wanted to do something to help but didn't know what. "Why are you bleeding?"

"I've been shot." I couldn't worry about the way her eyes went wide at those words. I had to get backup called in case whoever was outside had friends. Blood ran down my hand as I pulled up Alder's number and hit call, putting the phone on speaker so I didn't have to hold it up.

Alder answered right away. "What's up, Gage?"

"Handgun with a laser sight, close range. They were aiming for Katie. We need backup."

"Fuck. We're on our way."

"He's shot," Katie yelled, sounding way more collected than she should have been. "They shot him in the arm, and he's bleeding pretty bad."

Pretty bad was a relative term. "It's not that—"

"We're coming, Katie. Keep pressure on the wound to slow the blood loss, okay?" I heard the slam of car doors in the background. "Do you know how to shoot?"

Oh, fuck no.

"She won't need to. I'll keep her safe. Just haul ass." I ended the call before pressing the phone into Katie's hand, which trembled in mine. "What's the code?"

"I don't remember. Gage, I'm so sorry we fought—"

"Focus and remember. We'll deal with the rest later. Right now, I need to make sure you can call for help. The code...think about it."

She made a sound like a whimper. Still shaking. Still looking so scared. "Gage, that's a lot of blood."

"Doesn't matter, what's the code?"

"Gage, I don't—"

"It's your name, Katie." Pain shot across my back, a fire burning under my skin. I needed to get her tucked away while I still had a chance to fight back against whoever was on the other side of the door. Get comfortable being uncomfortable was a SEAL motto of sorts—I was real fucking used to being uncomfortable, but this was beyond. This was the sort of pain that scrambled your brain. I was running on borrowed time.

"My name?"

"Yeah, 5284...it spells Katie minus the E. I need you to remember it because I won't be with you to unlock it. Can you do that for me?"

She whimpered, clinging harder to my hand as she darted another look at my shoulder. "Okay, 5284."

"Good. Now go hide in the closet in the master bedroom. It locks from inside, so get in there and secure the door. I need you safe."

She didn't move, though. "You can't fight anyone alone—you've been shot."

"Yeah, well...it's not the first time." I pushed up from the floor, wishing the room would stop spinning so I could get my bearings. "Go now, Katie. They could be at the door any second."

Thankfully, she got to her feet. "They could shoot you through the glass."

"They're bulletproof."

"What?"

"My windows—they're all bulletproof. They'd have to have some serious ammunition to get through them." I shoved her down the hallway, the sound of footsteps outside fueling my harshness with her. No fucking way were they getting her. Not on my watch.

"Gage, stop—"

I pushed her right into the closet, knowing there were things left unsaid between us. Some that needed saying...just in case. "I'm not them, Katie. They demanded and overpowered you to do you harm. I do it to keep you safe. You want to go? Fine, but not until I know whatever threat is waiting for you outside this cabin has been taken care of. Now, lock the fucking door, and don't open it until Alder gets here. Not even for me unless I call you princess. Understand?"

She nodded, looking terrified. Something that would haunt me for the rest of my days. But I still had one more thing left to say. Just a few more sentences she needed to hear.

"I love you, princess. I'm sorry I didn't show you the way I should have, but that doesn't change the way I feel. It also doesn't change the fact that if it was your...the sheriff who sold you out, I'm going to kill him because I won't let a threat to you strike a second time."

She never said a word, simply rushed at me, pressing her lips to mine in a hungry kiss as Rex began barking madly. And fuck, did her body hitting mine hurt, but I'd take that pain any day.

I had to break the kiss way too soon—hard not to when I heard my dog jumping at the front window. Company was on the porch. "Lock the door, remember?"

"I will. And my name on the phone. Gage, please—"

"Alder's on his way. Do you know how to shoot?" At her nod, I pulled out the footlocker I kept my weapons in, entered the combination to unlock it, threw open the lid and grabbed a second gun—a Beretta M9 semiautomatic with a fifteen-round magazine and a suppressor. Just in case. Then I showed her what was inside. "You feel threatened, grab something out of here that looks familiar, okay? They're all loaded. I'll be back for you as soon as I clear the threat."

I gave her one final kiss, closed the footlocker, and then I walked out of the closet, shutting the door behind me, and headed for the living room. Pain forgotten. Training in place and fueling my stride. No fucker was taking my house or my woman —didn't matter how many holes they put in me. I'd protect what was mine so long as I had breath in my lungs.

Just as I reached the end of the hall, the front door blew open, knocking Rex across the room and sending pieces of wood flying. Not a gunshot, not a kick—a goddamned explosive had just gone off on my porch. Someone wanted to play with the big boys?

Game time.

Chapter Eighteen

KATIE

Staying locked in the closet while knowing Gage was out there with some sort of enemy attacker for a second time was a lot harder than the first. Hard enough that I lasted all of about two minutes. I hadn't planned to go against Gage's orders —in fact, I'd fully intended to follow them to the letter. Right up until something that sounded like a bomb went off in the house. Followed closely by a volley of gunshots that ended faster than I would have expected. Every thought I had, every emotion and memory and idea disappeared. My entire being focused down to one single question.

What if Gage was already dead?

A visceral sort of boiling started in my blood, an anger that completely overtook me. No way would I leave him to deal with whatever was coming on his own. He'd said backup was on the way, but that didn't mean they'd get to us in time. Or that he had cast a wide enough net when he'd asked for help. He'd only called Alder, and though the oldest Kennard had said *we* in return, I didn't know what that *we* included. Gage had told me last time that if he went down, I was to contact everyone in his phone to help me.

Gage was the one who needed help, and that list was where we'd find it.

I unlocked Gage's phone, nearly tearing up as I spelled out my own name on the keypad—my silly, sentimental beast of a man—before opening his contact list. But there was a surprisingly small number of names in his phone. Looking over the list, I knew all but two of them. I skipped the guys who worked for him and the other mill workers I recognized. I also passed right over Camden, knowing he likely wouldn't be coming back to Justice anytime soon even if someone he once considered a friend needed him. That left me with five male names including Alder who was already on his way. This wouldn't be news to him, but the update might make him drive faster. Thumbs typing extra quick and second thoughts banished so I didn't change my mind, I wrote a group text to Alder, Bishop, Deacon, Finn, and someone named Parris.

"Here goes nothing."

At Gage's cabin. He's been shot, and there was an explosion. HURRY.

But sending a message for more help wasn't enough. Gage had already been injured when he'd walked out the door. I had his blood on my shirt, on my hands. I couldn't let him face down the men who were there because of me all alone. I needed to be his backup until someone with more experience and skill could take over for me.

With shaking hands, I rushed to open the footlocker Gage had pulled his gun from. Inside, there were more weapons than

I'd ever seen in one place, most of them useless to me because I didn't know how to shoot or load them. But there was one I was familiar with—a shotgun. I'd grown up enjoying the outdoors. Had learned to hunt and to shoot when I was still a preteen. I'd fired a shotgun, a skill that might just come in handy.

I lifted the gun from inside, frowning at the barrel. It was far shorter than I was used to—made of what looked like stainless steel with a black stock and forend—but otherwise, it looked just like the guns I'd gone out into the woods with all those years ago. I checked the magazine tube to make sure it was loaded and found six slugs. I went ahead and released the action to pump the shotgun and chamber the first round, then disengaged the safety. I wasn't sure what sort of ammunition I needed for it, so I didn't grab extra, but I figured six shots were better than nothing.

Anything to save Gage.

Anything to give me a second chance to clean up the mess he'd made by not telling me what was going on.

Of course, I had secrets too. Ones that I needed to tell him—things he should know so he could understand the full picture of Sheriff Mark Baker. And I would...as soon as we got the hell out of the danger zone and patched him up.

Gage might have been sneaky about getting the information he needed, but he'd done that to protect me. We could talk about his methods and what I deemed as damaging to my trust once we were safe, and we would. The man loved me—the least I could do was make sure he lived long enough to know that I loved him too and that we would find a way to work this out.

But first, we needed to destroy the enemy. Clear the threat, as Gage would say. I threw open the closet door, gun in my hands and resolve in my bones. Noises came from the living room, the sound of deep, masculine voices arguing, though the lack of Rex's throaty bark struck me as odd. I really hoped that silly mutt was okay—I'd gotten a bit attached to him. I couldn't lose Gage, but the thought of losing Rex? Of the heartbreak that would cause my mountain man? It made me ache almost as much.

Breathe, Katie.

"Gage. It's all about Gage." I took a deep breath, and I walked out the bedroom door.

You can do this. You have to. At least, that's what I kept telling myself as I crept down the hallway, the recoil pad of the shotgun up against my shoulder and my finger sitting really close to the trigger. Ready to fire. Ready to do anything to make sure Gage kept breathing right along with me. I was a Colorado girl—I could shoot, I could hunt, and if the prey happened to be human for once, well... I could do what needed to be done to protect my man.

Just as soon as I stopped shaking.

Gage's voice reached my ears first, sending a wave of relief over me. At least he was alive. And pissed off, by the sound of it.

"She's your niece."

Which meant Mark was out there. A fact confirmed a second later.

"She's a means to an end. The Soul Suckers want to teach Justice a lesson, and what could be better than taking one of their own daughters from them?" That voice was something from my nightmares—cold and harsh. Cruel. A tone I'd only heard once before from him. One that used to wake me up from a sound sleep and leave me screaming. *Sit still, and it'll stop hurting. I can make you feel good if you'd just stop fighting me.*

A chill swept over my body, and I trembled from head to toe. That day, that memory, was the worst I'd ever lived through. It had been the catalyst for a lot of change—new city, new school, new life far away from the home I'd always loved. It was something I'd never spoken about outside of when I'd told my mom what had happened, something I'd never truly gotten over.

But I would not throw up before I even made it down the hallway.

"And you, right?" Gage said, sounding way more exhausted than I would have liked. "Because they wouldn't be going after your family if you hadn't fucked up somehow. What was it—the loss of men since they decided to try to take on Justice? How many are missing now...seven? Eight? Must not look good that you can't control one tiny little town in your county. I bet they see this as all your fault—you were probably the one who told them to set up that meth lab out on the ridge. That's it, isn't it? You tried to give them Justice, not realizing you didn't have the pull to hand it over."

Deep down, I wanted my uncle to argue that. To tell Gage he was wrong. As a little girl, I'd loved the man and assumed he'd loved me. I'd learned the hard way this his form of love wasn't a healthy one, but there was still a five-year-old Katie inside of me wanting to see the good side win.

But instead of an argument, I got a confirmation of how much he wasn't the man I'd grown up thinking he was. Not that I really needed another lesson in that.

"Fuck you, Shepherd."

Yeah. That sounded like a confirmation for sure. Something Gage must have heard as well.

"Hit the nail on the head, didn't I? The Soul Suckers—your meth-selling, biker gang *brothers*—see you as being responsible for all these losses they're taking because you told them Justice would be a good place to set up shop. That's why they opened a clubhouse just over the county line—to keep a crew close enough to watch their business, but not in your county. You turned a blind eye to the meth lab while they did most of their dirty work in someone else's jurisdiction. And now, because you fucked up big-time with that recommendation, you've got a debt to pay. You're giving them your own flesh and blood to smooth things over. That's pretty fucking sick, man. Real brothers would never even think of such a thing. They'd go all out to protect your family, not destroy it. I wonder what the punishment will be when you come back empty-handed. You think you'll walk away from that, or will they fucking bury you?"

Gage sounded all sorts of wrong to me. Not as bold or strong, not as overwhelming. Talking way too much for someone who was normally more the strong, silent type. I didn't know if Mark would have spent enough time with him to tell how off the man sounded, but I could. And the idea that Gage was somehow losing ground—that his strength was slipping away—terrified me.

"Katie's coming with me," Mark said. "She's safest with me. They'll let her go once Alder is dealt with."

"That's a big negative on all of that. Katie's not going anywhere, and if they keep coming for Alder or anyone else in this town, we'll keep taking them out." Gage must have moved because the floor creaked just a little. Enough to tell me pretty much where he was. Right in front of the end of the hallway— guarding the only path to the bedroom where I'd been hiding. Of course.

"Big words from a man who can't even stand up."

My heart nearly stopped. Gage...unable to stand up? Impossible. The man was a force of nature—a big, strong boulder of a human being. If he was down, things were much worse than I'd thought.

Not that he'd let Mark know that. "I can still kick your ass from the floor, old man."

But he shouldn't have to—and I wouldn't let him try. I hurried the rest of the way into the living room, aiming straight at the man I'd once called uncle as I turned the final corner. As I moved next to Gage, who was indeed sitting on the floor at the head of the hallway, blocking the only path to me. Pointing his handgun at Mark with his left hand. His right arm was covered in blood, as was his left leg. Jesus, he'd been shot a second time. Something I couldn't even think of at that moment or else I wouldn't be able to do what needed to be done.

Clear the threat.

"How come I always seem to miss the fun?" I stepped between Gage and Mark, keeping my shotgun leveled on the not-so-good sheriff. Refusing to let the sight of him take me back to that place. That moment. That car. "Hey, Mark. I'd ask how you're doing, but I really don't give a fuck."

Gage whispered a harsh, "Katie—" but I shushed him, keeping all my attention on my so-called *uncle*. The man who'd torn out my heart with his cruelty. Who'd made me and my mom run away from the only home we'd ever known because of his abuse.

"You need to come with me, Katie. I'll take care of you now."

The man who was apparently delusional.

"Not happening."

"That's an order. I'm not just your uncle, I'm the county sheriff. Don't make me take you in on resisting arrest charges."

"That's not happening either."

"You're leaving me no choice, young lady." He raised his gun, sighting down the barrel as he pointed it at me. "Drop your weapon."

Feet shoulder-width apart, recoil pad mounted against my shoulder, both arms strong, finger on the trigger. Ready to shoot. "No."

"I've got friends outside, Katie. You come with me, and I can protect you. I can claim ownership of you so they don't lay a hand on you."

"Damn it, Katie." Gage groaned and shifted closer to me, but I was too focused on Mark to pay attention to anything else.

"As if you'd be any better? Or did you forget? Do I need to punch you in the balls again to remind you of what you did to me, *Uncle Mark*?"

He shot a glance at Gage, looking slightly less confident for just a moment. That memory really must have been a hard hit to his whole "big, strong man" persona. His little niece had dropped him with one punch. I'd been a kid then, a high school girl, and I'd beaten him. I'd struck hard and gotten away when he'd tried to control me. Tried to take what wasn't his. When he'd pinned me against the door in his cruiser and attempted to rip off my clothes, claiming that I needed to do what he said because I was *his little Katie*.

I wasn't his little anything and never had been.

He still didn't see that, though. "Katherine Renee Baker, you listen to your uncle."

"Fuck you. Drop your gun, or I'll shoot."

His arrogant smile sent a chill up my spine. One I wouldn't let overpower me or make me run scared. I had this. I *had* this.

"You'll go to jail if you do."

I knew enough about the men in this town to know that likely wouldn't happen. I'd run home to Justice for a reason, and he wasn't it.

Still, I cocked my head as I said, "Hey, Gage?"

"Yeah, princess?" His voice cracked, sounding breathy and tired. This needed to end.

"It's just the three of us here, right?"

"That'd be my guess. He can bluff all he wants, but if he had friends with him, they'd be inside already." He shifted a little closer, his shoulder brushing against my leg. "Why?"

"Well, I was thinking. See, my mom and I ran from Justice because good old Uncle Mark here thought he could put his hands on me without getting into trouble. We couldn't really go to the police since he *was the police*, and my mom was too kindhearted to kill her own brother." I turned my head, watching Mark. Pinning him with my stare. "I'm not as nice as she was. The way I see it, if it's just the three of us here, then there are no witnesses to whatever happens next. Are you going to tell the good people of the county that I shot Sheriff Baker here?"

"Not a fucking chance."

Mark just laughed. "You don't have the backbone."

"You doubt me. I wouldn't if I were you. I've been planning your murder since the day you shoved your fingers inside me and told me to sit still so you could make me *feel good*. You remember that day, *Uncle*? Because I do. I remember it every time I have a nightmare that you've somehow gotten me alone again. I remember it every time I have to get in a car with a man alone. I remember, and I hate you just a little bit more for every single time that memory steals my breath." I shrugged, fighting to control the way my entire body trembled under his gaze as Gage practically growled at my feet. "I'm done remembering. A little bleach, a couple of good knives, and a pig farm. That's all I need to make sure no one ever finds out what happened to you."

Mark scowled, lifting his gun and looking ready to kill. "Drop your goddamned weapon, girl."

"No. You don't get to tell me what to do. Ever."

I caught the flicker of his eyes, the way he glanced down at Gage. I didn't need to see his arms lower to know what was coming, to figure out his plans. If he couldn't get me to do what he wanted, he'd go for Gage, assuming I'd drop my weapon to protect him. To take care of him. I'd been a nurturer my entire life, had followed all the rules and done what I was supposed to at every turn. Except when it came to the man behind me.

So I firmed up my stance.

And I tightened my hold on the shotgun.

And I almost screamed when a strong body came up behind me, locking their arms around me as they reached forward to put their left hand over my right one. To hold me in place with the shotgun still against my shoulder. To press his finger against mine and squeeze the trigger.

To shoot the man standing before me so I didn't have to.

The recoil pushed me against Gage's hard body, and the blast made my ears ring. I kept my feet, though. Kept my eyes open to watch what we'd done. To see the nightmare of my past get what he deserved. Gage dropped his arm around my waist, pulling me to the side as my uncle fell. As his blood splattered and he dropped to the floor, his eyes lifeless.

Dead.

Because of us.

Oh god. "Gage."

"I've got you, Katie." But he didn't. In fact, he barely seemed to have himself. He slipped lower along the wall, taking me with him, falling to the floor in a slow glide that almost defied gravity. Landing in a heap of bone and muscle, but no spirit. No consciousness.

No Gage.

"Gage, no," I cried, trying to pull him over. To turn him. To reach his right shoulder so I could put pressure on his wound as Alder had told me to. "Please, Gage. I can't move you. I need your help."

Nothing. No response.

Oh god. "Please, please, please. Don't do this now. Please don't die on me."

And still...nothing.

No Rex.

No Gage.

The threat had been cleared, and yet I had nothing.

Just nothing.

Chapter Nineteen

GAGE

Gunshot wounds were bullshit, and the pain from them could fuck right off. End of story.

Chapter Twenty

KATIE

We didn't take Gage to a hospital. Alder said there would be too many questions if we did because of the gunshot wound, so we took him to the private offices of some doctor Deacon knew instead. We, as in Bishop and I. Alder and Deacon...well, they had the body of a sheriff to deal with.

A sheriff Gage had killed so I didn't have to.

Protecting me right to the end.

I stroked Rex's coat, needing to keep the pup close to me. Bishop had found him unconscious at Gage's cabin and brought him with us. The poor thing had seemed groggy and a little off, but he'd been able to walk and had stayed right by my side all night. Which was just what I'd needed—he was my only tangible link to the man currently under the doctor's care. The man who'd risked his life and his freedom for me.

I couldn't even begin to think about what that all meant. "Think this is going to come back at him?"

Bishop didn't need me to explain what *this* I was asking about. "I doubt it. Alder and Deacon are going to handle cleanup, and they know what they're doing."

"Are they the best at it?"

He glanced at me, his expression screaming that he hadn't expected me to ask that question. "No."

Of course not. "Because Gage is." A quick nod confirmed my suspicion. "You guys do this often?"

"What do you think?"

I didn't know what to think. Not really. But then I thought of Gage—my wild mountain man. The sweetness inside of him and the care he took with me. The protective streak that could obliterate the sun with its size.

Even though he'd killed, I'd never call him a murderer.

"I think you're all very good men who sometimes have to do very bad things to keep people safe. But you do them for the right reasons."

"We do. That I can promise you." Bishop sat back, looking me over. Assessing me with an unnerving gray stare. "That dog is trying to protect you even though he can't keep his eyes open."

I smiled down at the shaggy mess half lying across my lap. "He's a good dog."

"That he is." Bishop sighed, sounding much more serious when he said quietly, "Alder thinks you fired the kill shot."

"I would have, but Gage did it instead." I shivered as I remembered his big body surrounding mine, the quiet way he simply took over. The feel of his hand covering mine. The pressure of his finger squeezing mine against the trigger. "He probably thought I was too afraid to go through with it."

Bishop laughed, the sound almost echoing in the shabby little office waiting room. "I doubt that. Knowing Gage, he probably thought killing a member of your own family would leave a scar too deep to get over, so he took that on for you."

That sounded more like Gage—a protector to a fault. And being that I had his best friend sitting next to me, someone who probably knew the man better than anyone else, I figured a few questions were in order. I scratched Rex behind the ears as I asked, "He'll always do that, won't he?"

"Do what?"

"Jump in and take over to keep me from being hurt."

"Yes." No pause, no question, no other option. That yes might as well have been a shackle of responsibility clamped on to Gage's body.

I huffed. "I hate that."

"Hate that he cares about you so much he'd do anything to protect you?"

How could I say yes to that? "Well..."

"Because that's what it is. A love big enough to block out everything else, every rule and guideline and law. I know we can be a little much—Anabeth makes sure to remind me of that every single day"—a cocky sort of grin pulled at his face—"but we can't help it. And why would you want us to? Gage would rather die than see you hurt, and that's not a bad thing."

It wasn't. Still, Gage hadn't exactly been completely altruistic. "His tactics could use a little refinement."

"As could his wardrobe. Have you seen that green flannel shirt he wears? The thing should have been retired a decade ago at least."

"Are you really complaining about his clothes?"

"He bitches about my shoes, so yes. I am." He leaned forward, resting his elbows on his knees. Growing serious once more. "Look, Katie. Gage is my best friend, closer to me than some of my brothers. I know just about everything about him, including how much he cares about you. I don't want to overstep here or say something I shouldn't, but I'll give you this. He's been alone and dealing with just us guys for a long time. If he needs refinements, refine him. I know Anabeth smooths some of my rough edges, and Shye certainly keeps Alder from being a total grump."

I might not have spent as much time around Anabeth and Bishop, but I had around Shye and Alder. I knew exactly how she kept him even-keeled. "That she does."

"With Gage, it's your turn. If you care for him even half as much as he does for you, put a little time in. Right now, he's like a piece of coal—squeeze him hard enough, and he'll turn into a diamond."

"Somehow, I doubt that."

"Me too, but it sounded damn good in my head."

I would have laughed, but at that moment, the doctor opened the door leading to the back where they'd taken Gage. Bishop and I both stood, his face just as serious as I knew mine had to be. Our shoulders brushing as we faced Gage's fate.

The doctor looked right at me, not even giving Bishop a glance before launching into his spiel. "He's okay, though there's some damage to his shoulder that's more than I should be handling. He's going to need to rehab that joint the same way he did the first time, but it might take longer to get full use back. Shot twice in almost the exact same spot—it's practically unheard of."

Bishop huffed a laugh. "The man is nothing if not consistent. First, he dives in front of a bullet to protect me, then he dives in front of a bullet to protect her."

The doctor pushed up his glasses. "Yes, well. Perhaps he should stop being so brave."

Bishop bumped me with his elbow. "That'll never happen."

I wasn't ready to joke just yet, though. "What about his leg? He was shot in the leg, too."

"Through and through. Minimal damage and a clean wound."

"That sounds...okay?" I glanced at Bishop, who nodded. "What else?"

The doctor gave me a small smile. "He's going to be in a lot of pain, so I'm going to write a prescription in your name for some pain medications. If anyone questions it, I want you to say it's for a partial tubal ligation you had done. Okay?"

I was going to have to lie to protect Gage...I didn't miss the irony of that. "Sure. Whatever I have to do."

"Good. He'll need to take them every four hours at first. They'll make him sleepy and foggy, but they'll help keep the pain to a minimum so he can rest and begin to heal. They won't take all of it away, though. If he needs something stronger, call me, and we'll figure something out. Hopefully, in a few weeks, the pain will subside, he'll be able to start rehabbing that arm, and you'll have your husband back."

"Oh," I said as heat rushed up my neck and face. "I'm not his—"

"She's his." Bishop shrugged when I darted a look his way. "You are. You'll figure it out eventually."

Yeah, I probably would. And until then, I'd take care of him because if I was his, that meant he was mine. "Okay, so I've got a handle on the pain management. What sort of symptoms or signs should I be watching for in regards to infection?"

Chapter Twenty-One

GAGE

I woke up to a screaming pain in my shoulder and the sounds of banging and running water coming from somewhere nearby. None of which I'd been expecting. I didn't even recognize the room I was in at first—at least not until the pain subsided enough for me to remember Bishop half carrying me up the stairs to Katie's apartment.

Her apartment, her room, her bed. *Fuck me.*

That would explain the noises coming from beyond the closed bedroom door, then. Katie had to be cooking. I rolled over and glanced at her alarm clock—three in the morning. My girl was cooking in the middle of the night, which meant something was wrong. Considering she'd been attacked again, had seen me pass out after being shot twice, and had watched me murder her uncle, that wasn't a bit surprising.

I crawled out of bed, the burning in my chest and neck nothing compared to the deep, throbbing pain in my arm. I needed a fucking pain pill, but I also needed a clear head. At least for a few minutes. Which was probably all I'd get because the pain would knock any sense I could scrounge together out of my head soon enough—more than the pills would. I needed to track down my girl and make sure she was okay before my brain turned to mush again.

I found Katie in the kitchen just as I'd expected, her hair pulled up in a messy bun and her legs covered in those sexy as sin not-really-pants I loved so much. I'd like to have said my dick responded to the sway of her ass in those skintight black things, but it didn't. My body was probably too focused on the agony tearing through my right side to give any thought to my Johnson.

Tragic.

"What are you doing?"

Katie spun, looking surprised and scared. Of me. Fuck, I needed to tone it down.

"Sorry. I just meant...it's a weird time to be cooking."

"I couldn't sleep. Are you hungry?"

Always. For her. But right then, that wasn't the question. "Maybe some toast or something. If you don't mind."

Her smile and the way she seemed to relax right there in front of me stole my breath. "I don't mind."

She turned to bend over—*lord have mercy, that ass will be the death of me*—and grabbed the bread from a cabinet while I settled onto one of the little stools along her counter. My leg didn't hurt nearly as bad as my shoulder, but lifting it to place my foot on the rungs of the stool certainly pulled a little. I was a mess. I was also without my shadow.

"Where's Rex? I remember him flying across the room when the grenade went off, but then—"

"He's fine," she said, probably knowing the thought of losing my dog would be a harsh one. "He got knocked around a bit, but nothing's broken. Bishop and Anabeth are keeping him for a few days. I figured that was better than dealing with him here because Alder doesn't want me outside alone right now. He's worried about retaliation from the Soul Suckers for...what happened."

What happened...which was Katie and me facing down Mark Baker. Though the final memories of that standoff weren't quite clear. "Did I kill the sheriff or did you?"

She froze, her finger just about to depress the lever for the toaster, her voice going a little softer as she answered, "You did."

At least I'd gotten one thing right. "Good."

"I was going to, you know."

Of that, I had no doubt. "I know, but I couldn't let you do that. Even if he deserved it for what he did to you."

She held my gaze, her expression flat. Guard up. "I should have told you—"

"If we have to rehash all the things we should have told each other, we'll be here all night."

"I knew he'd come after me, though."

That was something I hadn't expected. "You did?"

"It's why we left Justice. My mom knew there'd be no stopping him. That day...after I got away from him...I went home and told her what he'd done. What he'd been trying to do for a long time."

"Katie—"

"Let me finish," she said, looking so small and scared but putting on a brave face. One that relaxed a little when I nodded at her to continue. "I never realized how much interference my mom ran when he was around. Always staying with the two of us, never wanting him to be alone with me. As a kid, I just thought the extra attention was because he cared about me. I didn't realize how much he didn't until it was almost too late."

The idea of that fucker around a young, innocent Katie set

my blood boiling. "I wish I could kill him all over again for hurting you."

Her smile, as weak as it was, still lit up the room. "I know, but it could have been so much worse. My mom never doubted me. That day, when I came running home with my clothes torn and blood dripping down my thighs, she didn't even have to ask who'd done that to me."

"But there was no one to tell." I grabbed on to the edge of the counter, needing to hold myself in place. To stay steady so she could tell me what she needed to before I blew the fucking world down. He'd made her bleed? If I'd have known that, there would have been no plan, no plot, and no strategy. I would have walked right up to him in the street and put a bullet in his head. Add in the fact that he'd used his position—his so-called power—to control Katie and her mom, and there was no doubt the man had gotten what he'd deserved.

Justifiable homicide had never been more accurate.

Katie wasn't through with her story, though. "He'd just gotten voted in as our sheriff. He'd been covering things up and doing shady stuff with shadier people for years at that point—my mom knew anything we tried to pin on him would roll right off. So instead, we ran."

"Right after he...the car?" She'd lived it, and I couldn't even say it. Motherfucker, did my girl have a will of pure steel.

"That same day. She packed up what we could fit in our car, and we headed to Denver."

Apparently, Katie took after her mother. "Brave woman."

"She was—and protective. She would have hated me coming back to Justice—to his county—but I had to. I always felt safe here, even with him looming in the distance." She locked eyes with me, giving me the most serious, weighted look I'd ever seen. "I still do."

As she should. "I'd do anything to keep you safe."

"I know that, but I'm not weak."

"I never said you were."

"I don't always need you to protect me."

"Too bad."

She blinked, my words pulling her up short. "Excuse me?"

"I said, too bad." I rose from my stool, moving around the edge of the little bar. Closing in on her. "You think I wanted to see your face after you murdered your uncle right there in my living room? No fucking way. You think I could live with myself if I had to clean up your blood from the floor after someone shot you like he shot me? Not happening. And if you think there's even a chance I wouldn't throw myself in front of you again to stop anyone from hurting you in any way, you don't know me at all." I herded her against the counter, running a finger softly along her cheek when I had her pinned where I wanted her. "I protect you not just because it keeps *you* safe, but because I'm a selfish bastard who doesn't want to give you up. Ever."

She didn't look convinced. "You lied to me."

"And I'll never forgive myself for that. It really did seem like the right thing to do at the time, but I can see where I went wrong." I licked my lips, leaning closer. Wishing I could taste her just for a second. That I'd earned back the right to. But we weren't there quite yet. "I figure shit out and get the jobs done. That's always been my thing. I'm not used to having to worry about people trusting me and how those jobs affect that."

"Well, you need to now," she said, bringing her hands to my chest. "Because I won't be with someone I don't trust."

Her touch almost made the pain go away. Almost. "That sounds like you might not be walking away from me, princess."

She snorted a sarcastic sound, inching closer. Bringing her hot little body against mine. "You think I'd walk away from you after that whole "I love you" speech in the closet?"

"I don't know. Just because I love you doesn't mean you have to return the feeling. You might be willing to leave me behind." Though, I'd die if she did. Or die trying to win her back. Either one.

Thankfully, my death didn't seem necessary. "Never."

"You saying you've got feelings for me?"

"Maybe." She locked her big, hazel eyes with mine, giving me so much hope even as she threatened me with, "But if you lie to me again, we're going to have some serious issues."

I'd take her maybe over a hell no any day. "Understood."

"Good." She turned around, teasing me with that ass pressing against my uncooperative cock. "Now, eat your toast. It's about time for your medicine."

I scowled, leaning down to wrap my arms around her waist and rest my head on her shoulder. "They make me sleep too much."

"They're supposed to."

They were. Didn't mean I had to like it, though. "You coming to bed with me?"

She turned back around with a plate of toast in her hand, her expression torn. "I don't want to hurt you worse."

"Walking away would have hurt me worse. Cuddling up with you—even with my bad shoulder—is nothing in comparison."

"You and your sweet words." She took a deep breath, frowning as she set the plate on the counter. Looking nervous all of a sudden. "I'm not as good with words as you are, even when you don't use any. You can stand there completely silent and say more than I do with a thousand ridiculous sentences—"

"Your sentences aren't—"

She put a finger against my lips, shushing me softly. "I need to get this out, so please just allow me to babble."

I slid my hands down to grip her hips, pulling her with me as I leaned against the counter, and nodded. "Go for it."

She took a deep breath, clutching my T-shirt tighter as if needing something to hold on to. "You use words sparingly, and that's okay. But what you say with them, the meaning behind them, carries so much more weight because of that. I don't want you to think that mine aren't as serious just because I use so many, so I'm getting them all out now before I get to what I really want to say."

She stared up at me, the most adorable, intense expression on her face. "Gage Shepherd, I know you love me, and I know you want to protect me. But all that goes both ways because I love you too, and I'll always—*always*—have your back."

I waited a full five seconds after those last words—the longest goddamned five seconds in my life—before asking, "Are you done?"

"Yes."

"Good." And then I took her mouth with mine, kissing her harder than I should have, tangling my tongue with hers as my heart practically exploded out of my chest.

"Gage," she gasped when I finally let her go, which wasn't really what I wanted to do. So I kissed her again, a smaller, sweeter one. Taking a taste of her. Holding on to the woman I loved— who somehow loved me right back—with every bit of strength I had.

Which wasn't much.

"That was to shut you up," I said, grinning against her lips when I had to stop. "There's a fuckton of words I need to say, but I'm usually enjoying listening to yours too much to remember to say them. But this time..." I dropped to my knees in front of her, needing to not be towering over her when I made my admissions. When I babbled, Katie-style. "The day after I met you that first time, I threw out half a refrigerator full of food because I knew I wouldn't be eating it. I'd be at The Baker's Cottage every day instead, just to get the chance to see you. And I pulled every guard duty assignment for Main Street that I could, not because I felt obligated, but because I didn't want to take my eyes off you. Every bit of research I did on your uncle was to keep you safe, but I should have told you about it. I should have asked you myself, and for that, I'm truly sorry. It won't happen again. And I gave you access to my GPS signal in good faith, but I'll be honest—if I'm working a job that might put you in danger if you know about it, I won't have my phone on me. Oh, and the gun that Rock stole from me? I got it back already. Don't ask me how or what happened because I don't want any shit coming your way, but it's nothing to worry about anymore. That's all my truths, save one. You're my light, my princess, and I love you more than I ever thought possible, which is why I *have* to protect you."

"You *don't* have to protect me."

If only she knew how untrue that was. "I do have to—not because you're weak. You're anything but. I have to protect you because if I lost you, I'd never recover. You're mine, but only because you allow me the honor of having you. I'm yours either way, and nothing's ever going to change that."

She stood silent for a long time, looking down at me. Practically trembling against me. Finally, she whispered, "Gage?"

"Yeah, Katie?"

"Eat some damned toast and take your medicine so we can go to bed."

I grinned up at her. "Is that an order?"

"Yes."

"Good. I like taking orders from you."

She reached behind her and handed me the plate with the toast on it. But instead of taking it, I grabbed her and pulled her closer. Tucked myself against her curvy little body and clutched her to me with my head resting against her chest. "When I heal up, I'm going to spend an entire afternoon doing nothing but teasing that pretty cunt of yours with my tongue."

She gripped me tighter, her eyes going unfocused. "That sounds nice."

"Oh, princess, there'll be nothing nice about it. I'm going to lay you down and spread those thighs wide. Pin you to the bed so you're on display just for me." I rose to my feet and kissed her, flicking my tongue against hers the way I longed to do to her little clit. The way that made her arch and gasp and cry my name. "And when you're through—not me, because I could eat you for days —I'm going to sink inside you nice and deep. Fuck you slowly on that bed of yours. Make you shudder and scream just for me. You want me to do all that?"

Her answer was an immediate, "Yes."

So I would.

"Give me the fucking toast. I want you naked and wrapped around me in two minutes."

"No sex, though. Doctor's orders."

We'd see about that. The SEALs had taught me to get comfortable being uncomfortable. I figured I had a good forty minutes after I took my pain pills before the drugs knocked me on my ass again.

Plenty of time.

Epilogue

GAGE

Alder and Shye's wedding seemed really chaotic, though seeing as it was the first one I'd ever attended, I didn't have much to compare it to. I also doubted others would have seemed as harried considering I probably would have been a guest instead of the hired help.

"Put that pan over there, please." Katie pointed in the general direction of the bar area at The Baker's Cottage before racing toward the kitchen with my dog on her heels. Somehow since Katie had moved in to my cabin with me, I'd lost control of Rex. He'd become Katie's dog, following my girl around much like I did. Wanting to be with her every second of the day...again, much like I did.

I'd always said he was the smartest dog in the world—his love for Katie only proved that.

Mercy Bell, hardware store owner, single mom, and the person helping Shye coordinate the wedding, came striding through the restaurant with her clipboard in her hands. "We've got fifteen minutes to get everything done before it's dress time. Let's go, people."

I set the pan of appetizers where I hoped Katie wanted them and looked for my next task, because I knew there'd be one. My girl had been a basket case about this event for like three weeks. Ever since Alder announced he was marrying his girl in one hell of a quickie ceremony. Not as quick as Bishop had married his, though.

Speaking of Bishop...

"Hey, man," he said, walking up beside me. "Nice tie. Seventies vintage back in style?"

Jackass. "Katie bought me this tie, so you can fuck right off. Though I see you're wearing those flat-bottomed shoes again. I thought we talked about that."

"It's a wedding. You have to look nice."

Katie reappeared out of the kitchen, smiling when she saw me. My girl looked better than nice. She also looked like she was about to drop the large trays of food in her hands.

"Princess, let me." I rushed over, grabbing the pans from her hands. "Where do you want these?"

"Next to the others."

"Got any more back there? I can lend you Bishop."

"I'm here for you, Gaines," Bishop said, giving my girl a smile and using her original surname. She hadn't changed hers from Baker, but Bishop didn't care. He just liked seeing the smile that name put on her face. So did I. I guess he wasn't always a jackass. Just...most of the time.

"I'm fine, but thank you," Katie said, still looking anything but fine. "There are just so many timing issues with the menu Shye picked, and the appetizers really need to be heated through before they go into the chafing dishes, which was something I had hoped we wouldn't have to deal with. Not that I'm complaining, though, because I'm happy to make anything for her since she's getting married today, and I want it to be perfect. It's just a lot to plan and prepare, plus, I have to change and stand up in the wedding and try to look somewhat pretty in my dress—"

I grabbed her around the waist and lifted her right off the ground, pressing my lips to hers in a kiss that had her moaning in about two seconds. She was so sweet, as if she'd been taste testing the icing on the wedding cake. I couldn't stop licking into her mouth, going in for another treat. Another sample. Didn't help that she had her hands in my hair, tugging me closer with every breath. Making me want to throw her down right there on the floor of the restaurant and show her just how pretty I thought she was. Not that she didn't already know, especially in regards to her pretty pussy.

Bishop's laugh interrupted our moment, though. "Damn, you two, get a room."

I pulled back slowly, still holding Katie in my arms. Refusing to stop kissing her just because my best friend felt the need to interrupt us.

"Better?" I asked when she finally smiled up at me.

She licked her lips as if needing one last taste of mine. "I love it when you do that."

She didn't...not all the time, at least. But sometimes, when her nerves got the best of her, it was a good way to settle her down. Though it certainly didn't settle my dick. I was hard as stone right there at Alder's wedding—pretty sure he'd be pissed about that if he found out.

"I need to get these chafing dishes lined up real quick. It's almost dress time," Katie said after a moment, frowning.

I shook my head and kissed her again before setting her back on her feet. "Why don't you go get your dress on? I can take care of this."

She didn't look too convinced of that. "Are you sure?"

"Absolutely." I patted her ass. "Go. I know you want to help Shye get ready as well."

With a grin and a quick kiss goodbye, she raced off for the alley with Rex at her side. The girls were getting ready over at Katie's old apartment. We had men stationed in the alley and in both buildings just in case, though things had gotten awfully quiet for us since Sheriff Baker's body had been found.

Motorcycle clubhouses were hard to keep open when a law enforcement official's body was discovered on their property. Especially one that looked as if it had been dead for a few weeks. Funny thing—motorcycle clubs like the Soul Suckers didn't like cops, so when their members found a dead body in their parking lot, they tried to hide it. *Tried* being the operative word.

The entire body drop and framing had been an ingenious plan Deacon had come up with after the night I'd killed the good sheriff. He and Alder had taken care of hiding the body somewhere as they waited for their opportunity, then they'd disappeared for a couple of days to deal with Pistol—Shye's former stepbrother and the man leading the charge to get vengeance on her and the entire town of Justice.

I hadn't been involved in that plan, though, so I wasn't sure how those two had managed to take out the bastard without catching a lot of blowback from it. What I did know was that, if I ever needed a sneaky motherfucker to help me out, I was calling one of those two former Green Berets.

I also knew that the very next morning after the two returned home from their mission, Alder and Shye were engaged and planning the wedding happening in just under an hour. The man worked fast.

Again, not as fast as Bishop, though. He'd come home from Vegas last week with a ring on his finger, a wife on his arm, and a baby on the way. Luckiest bastard in the world, that one.

"Has anyone seen my wife?" Bishop asked, as if reading my mind and knowing I had been thinking about his Vegas wedding. He stood looking around the restaurant as if that leggy redhead would pop up out of a corner somewhere. I figured he just liked drawing attention to the fact that he already had a wife—he'd locked that shit down tight and fast. Faster than his older brother. A point of contention between the two that had led to some excellent mockery.

"She's probably over with the girls at Katie's old place," Deacon said as he strolled through the restaurant with a beer in one hand. "I've heard it's estrogenpalooza over there."

"Don't let the women hear you say that." Alder came up behind his best friend, grabbing his shoulders and smiling bigger than I'd ever seen him do before. "Everyone good? We need anything over here?"

I shrugged, not really needing anything but Katie. I pulled my phone from my pocket and shot her a quick text.

Naked yet?

It didn't take her long to reply.

Nope, though you're going to love this dress.

That caught my attention. *I want pics.*

Patience. Just look for the brunette in blue.

I don't need to know the color, princess. I'd spot those tits from across a sea of people in two seconds flat.

She replied faster than I would have expected. *Such a charmer.*

And all yours.

Always.

I grinned at that last text, knowing she meant it. We might not have made things as official as Bishop and Anabeth had, or

Alder and Shye were about to, but our commitment to each other was just as strong as theirs. Stronger, maybe. At least, in my opinion.

I looked up from my phone just as Finn headed our way. The former addict appeared good—healthy and strong. Clean. But I darted a glance in Bishop's direction just in case—there was still tension between the two brothers. A definite feeling of residual anger from Bishop because of Finn's role in Anabeth leaving him over a decade ago, even though Bishop had recently gotten his second chance with her. I understood the ire and had even backed Bishop up as he'd given his younger brother a little taste of what he'd deserved for those actions, but today wasn't the day for all that.

"Hey, guys," Finn said, reaching out to shake hands with each of us in turn. Even Bishop. "Congrats, Alder. I wish you and Shye the best."

"Thanks, man. Elijah and Lainie made it in yet?"

Finn's twin brother and the youngest Kennard and only girl in the family. "Yeah. They're coming right behind me." Finn turned to Bishop and gave him a careful sort of smile. "Congratulations to you as well. I wish you and Anabeth all the happiness in the world."

Bishop's smile wasn't as bright as it should have been, but it was there. "Thanks, Finn. I appreciate that."

Finn seemed to relax after that. "So...weddings and babies. You guys are getting old. Got your Viagra prescriptions yet?"

And that was how Finn ended up being chased out of The Baker's Cottage by his older brothers. Good times.

———

Katie hadn't been joking in her text—she looked fucking amazing in her dress. Low-cut, tiny little straps holding the fabric up over her full breasts, and a clingy sort of design that skimmed her hips just right. I loved it—I was going to love it even more when I ripped it off her to see what all was underneath it. If anything.

Bishop sat beside me, his arm around Anabeth and his hand resting on her belly. A family of three right there. Just the sort of life my best friend deserved. Finn, Elijah, and Lainie sat in front of us, the three youngest Kennards all looking on with smiles as their oldest brother married the woman of his dreams with his best friend by his side. Camden hadn't made it back to town for the event, but none of us had expected him to. There was a lot of anger and hurt still there. He'd come home when he was ready...at least, that was what we all hoped.

And me? I watched Katie. Not that anyone would have expected anything different from me. I was always looking at my girl. How could I not when she was so damn beautiful?

After the ceremony, I hunted down my girl in the kitchen of the restaurant.

"Hey," she said, grinning and looking ridiculously happy. "It was a beautiful ceremony, don't you think?"

I did, but that wasn't what I wanted to talk about. Between Bishop and Alder, I only had one thing on my mind. "You want this?"

Her smile turned a little questioning. "This what? The restaurant? Yes. You? Always." She tucked herself against my chest, rising up on the balls of her feet so she could press her lips to mine as she ran her hand over my beard. The one she'd trimmed again a few nights ago before dropping to her knees and taking me in her mouth. A great memory, but not my focus at the moment.

Later, absolutely.

"I like where you're going, princess, but I meant *this*. What Alder and Bishop have now. Rings and babies and all that."

Those hazel eyes I loved so much had never been wider. "Well, I mean, it's fast, isn't it? Though, I guess Alder and Shye were fast as well. But he loved her, like really really loved her. Not that you don't love me, but aren't guys more resistant to getting married? I don't know. I love you so much, and I think we're good together, but I don't want to mess anything up. I don't want to push you at all, so I—"

She deserved the kiss I planted on her lips. Not because she'd found herself having a nervous fit once again, but because she said she loved me. I could never resist her when she told me that.

Still, I didn't let the kiss go on for long because I really needed to get a straight answer from her. So I broke it, and I stared down at my entire world wrapped up in the sexiest package ever imagined, and I asked one last time.

"Do you want me, princess?"

No nervousness, no babbling. Just one word filled with more confidence than anything else she'd ever said before. "Yes."

I dropped down to my knees for her, exactly where I should have been. Where I belonged...being grateful for finding her and knowing exactly how fucking blessed I was. "Forever, princess? Tell me you want me forever."

She nodded, her smile growing wider. Filling me with so much love, I thought my chest might break open right there. Thought there was no way I could contain it all.

My girl. My world. Forever.

"You want me, then you'll have me. I'm an idiot for asking now because I don't have a ring or fancy words, but I have this—I will never stop loving you, Katie Baker Gaines. Not for a single second. Not now, not fifty years from now, not ever. I'm yours, baby. And I'd really like it if you'd be mine, too."

"I'll always be yours, Gage."

"Then let's get married. You and me...forever. Our lives bound together right here in Justice."

Never had anyone looked at me with more love than she did right then. "Yes. Let's get married. I want forever with you in Justice."

So she'd have it. Because nothing—not one goddamned thing —would ever come between me and my girl. Would ever threaten her happiness or her safety. Nothing bad would ever fucking touch her again.

Me and the men I saw as my brothers would make sure of it.

Acknowledgments

I got the final proofread copy of this book while staying in a hotel for the Chicago North RWA Spring Fling event. Damon Suede had given a presentation on branding that inspired me and a keynote that reminded me of the big picture not just in writing but in life. The incomparable Beverly Jenkins was there as well, and she took us to school on the issues surrounding being a woman of color in our industry. I have noting but love and thanks for them both and will forever be grateful for their words, their smiles, their openness, and their phenomenal dancing moves. Katie would approve.

Once again, Lisa Hollett with Silently Correcting Your Grammar had to put up with my crappy punctuation, my ridiculous typos (seriously—they're so bad sometimes), and text messages at all hours of the day. And she does it all with a tiara on her head, a glass of wine in her hand, and a smile on her face. At least she does in my imagination.

Franci Neill took her red pen to Gage and Katie's relationship, and lived to tell the tale. She's claimed Gage as her own—fair warning.

As for my Bitches™, there's no greater group of friends to be found. Trust me—I've looked. Row, bitch. Row.

Kristin Harte started off as a chemistry major in college but somehow ended up writing romances featuring ex-military heroes and the women who knock them to their knees...literally and figuratively. She likes drinking in the shade, snuggling under a warm blanket on a cold evening, and researching how to blow things up. Her children know nothing of what she writes, and her husband just hopes he's not at their Chicago-ish home the day the government shows up to confront Kristin about her Google search history.

When not writing good men doing bad things, Kristin can be found writing paranormal romance as Ellis Leigh, co-writing naughty novellas as London Hale, or taking her signature style into the mystery realm as Mille Thorne.

www.kristinharte.com
Kristin@KristinHarte.com

www.ingramcontent.com/pod-product-compliance
Lightning Source LLC
Chambersburg PA
CBHW050352190726
48284CB00007BB/2246